2000
Cinderella
Looking Back . . .

OTHER YEARLING BOOKS YOU WILL ENJOY:

EXPECTING THE UNEXPECTED, *Mavis Jukes*

PLANNING THE IMPOSSIBLE, *Mavis Jukes*

STRUDEL STORIES, *Joanne Rocklin*

THE RUNAWAYS, *Zilpha Keatley Snyder*

FROZEN SUMMER, *Mary Jane Auch*

YANG THE SECOND AND HER SECRET ADMIRERS,
Lensey Namioka

ONE-OF-A-KIND MALLIE, *Kimberly Brubaker Bradley*

WINTERING, *William Durbin*

THE BEADED MOCCASINS, *Lynda Durrant*

BUCKAROO, *Betty Traylor*

YEARLING BOOKS are designed especially to entertain and enlighten young people. Patricia Reilly Giff, consultant to this series, received her bachelor's degree from Marymount College and a master's degree in history from St. John's University. She holds a Professional Diploma in Reading and a Doctorate of Humane Letters from Hofstra University. She was a teacher and reading consultant for many years, and is the author of numerous books for young readers.

2000

Cinderella

Looking Back . . .

Mavis Jukes

A Yearling Book

Published by
Dell Yearling
an imprint of
Random House Children's Books
a division of Random House, Inc.
1540 Broadway
New York, New York 10036

Visit us on the Web! www.randomhouse.com/kids

Educators and librarians, for a variety of teaching tools, visit
us at www.randomhouse.com/teachers

ISBN: 0-440-22866-2

Reprinted by arrangement with Delacorte Press

Printed in the United States of America

January 2001

10 9 8 7 6 5 4 3 2 1

OPM

To my students at Hidden Valley,
Proctor Terrace and Steele Lane schools—
you guys are great.

Looking back...

Decomber 31, 1999: Where were you? And where were you on January 1, 2000? There's never been a more magical New Year's Eve than the one that occurred the night before the dawn of the new millennium.

For Ashley Ella Toral, it was the eve of the beginning of the rest of her life—and she'll remember it forever....

One

Two thousand silver helium balloons, with curled silver ribbons hanging down?

"You must be kidding!" said Ashley. She twirled the phone cord around her finger. "Two *thousand*?"

"That's what I heard . . . ," said Ana. "And there's going to be an ice sculpture in the middle of the buffet table: two, zero, zero, zero—with flower petals frozen in the numbers. But you *can't* tell anybody."

"I won't."

"It's a total secret."

"Fine," said Ashley. "But—who told you?"

"Emily. Brittany and Mara were talking about it in that new store next to Starr's. In the dressing room. They didn't realize Emily was trying on tops in the next booth."

"Oh."

"Emily hid in there till they left."

"Did she get any tops?"

"No. But she got a plastic tulip lamp." Ana paused. "Did your stepmom say you could get a new dress for the party? Or no."

"I've put off asking."

"Well, you'd better hurry up. The party's in two days!"

"I know," said Ashley. "But Phyllis's been saying she's all 'spent out' from Christmas . . . that the new couch and La-Z-Boy chair were really 'presents meant for *all* of us.' "

Ana grew quiet. "Well, if Phyllis *doesn't* say yes, remember: You really do look cute in your little black dress, Ashley."

"You think?"

"Mmmm-hmmm! Do you have shoes?"

"I can polish those little black strappy heels I got for Emily's Bat Mitzvah."

"They still fit?"

"I think so." But come to think of it, thought Ashley, I hope my toes don't hang over the edge.

Ashley heard a low rumbling sound. She lifted the curtain and looked out the window.

Yup.

Her stepmom was pulling in.

Ashley watched the ancient green station wagon lurch to a stop, barely missing one of the two dented garbage cans sitting on the side of the driveway.

"I have to go," Ashley told Ana. "Phyllis's home. And it's my turn for dishes—again."

"Talk to you later," said Ana.

They said goodbye and Ashley hung up the phone.

She spied on her two stepsisters as they got out of the car, each holding a shopping bag from Zil's. They left the car door open and strolled toward the front stoop. Ashley heard her stepmother shout, "Shut the car door!" but neither Paige nor Jessica responded.

"I mean it!"

"You!" yelled Paige. "We have to watch the soaps."

"You do not! One of you *shut that car door!*"

Words were exchanged; one sister swung her bag at the other. There was a brief scuffle, followed by a chase across the front yard.

Ashley let the curtain drop to the sill. She turned and surveyed the kitchen. The sink was half full of greasy water and piled with dirty dishes. A frying pan had been dunked and left to soak. A piece of fried egg was dangling from the handle.

There was even a stalk of celery floating in the water.

Ashley fished it out by one leaf and dropped it into the trash under the sink.

Ick! she thought.

She drained the sink and began to fill it again.

There was a loud thump at the front door, and Ashley heard a shout and giggles as her stepsisters raced down the hallway and slammed their bedroom door.

A moment later, Ashley's stepmother appeared in the kitchen. "You'll never guess," she said.

Ashley looked up. Phyllis's glasses were on top of her head, pulling back her hair and making two frightful wings.

"You guys went to the mall," said Ashley. "Again." She squirted some dishwashing liquid into the water and watched the bubbles rise.

"Right," said Phyllis. "We hit the sale at Zil's. The twins got velvet jumpers. And black dresses—similar to your black dress."

"*How* similar?" Ashley asked.

Phyllis shrugged. "Anyway, I've got news! My grammie has overcome her fear of flying! She's spontaneously decided to come out. And she's coming in guess when. Tomorrow afternoon! Can you believe it? I'm picking her up from the airport bus, right after I get off of work."

"You're not meeting her flight?"

"How?" said Phyllis. "You're on vacation, I'm not. That bum of a boss of mine has me working all the way up to four o'clock on New Year's Eve . . . like I don't have a life. But I have news for him and the rest of the world: My whole life's in front of me, not behind me. Right?"

"Right."

"And Grammie and I are going to ring in the new millennium with a bottle of French champagne she's been saving since 1984."

"Cool," said Ashley. She looked down at the suds filling the sink. "Where will she sleep?"

"Actually that's something we need to talk about," Phyllis began. She walked over to Ashley and put her arm around Ashley's shoulder. "It will only be for four nights," she whispered, giving Ashley a squeeze. "Thursday. Friday. Saturday. Sunday. Help me out here."

"She can't sleep in your bed with you? It's a king!"

"The woman's seventy-five years old," said Phyllis. "I think she's entitled to her own room, at *her* age."

Ashley picked up the dish brush and scrubbed at the little icky plugs of garlic stuck in the garlic press. She rinsed it and put it into the drain.

"The Christmas couch is really fluffy," said Phyllis in a cheery way. "And you can snuggle down in—in all those orange pillows."

"Can't the twins?" Ashley asked.

"Two? On one couch?"

"Well, what about one in a sleeping bag, on the floor? Or in the La-Z-Boy, tipped all the way back?"

"Sleep on the floor or in a chair? That wouldn't be fair. Would it?"

Ashley said nothing. It was plain that she would be giving up her room; it was pointless to discuss it. But hmmmm, she thought. Maybe now would be the moment . . .

Even though she was generally a jeans,

sweatshirts and sneakers girl, there was a streak of princess in Ashley. She looked down at the dishwater.

Steam was rising.

Imagine, she thought. You're floating into the New Millennium's Eve party, wearing high-heel shoes and a new dress, with part of your hair drawn up and fastened on top with a crown of rosebuds, each bud on an individual hairpin . . . or maybe just pulled back with some rhinestone clips . . . and the rest of your hair tumbling onto your shoulders and down your back.

Ashley popped her eyes open. Where was her body glitter? She hadn't seen it lately.

So much steam had risen from the sink, Ashley had practically given herself a facial. She quickly washed and rinsed the dishes, putting them neatly into the drain. "Phyllis?" she said. "Is there anything else you want me to do?"

Phyllis had wandered into the living room and was sorting through some bills. "Could you *please* come in here and talk to me? I don't like to talk room to room. You know that."

Ashley dried her hands on a dishtowel.

"Could I get a new dress for the New Millennium's Eve dance?" she quietly asked as she stood in the living room doorway. "I saw an ad in the paper for a huge post-Christmas sale at Starr's."

"Mom!" cried Jessica's voice from the other room.

"What!"

"Where's the remote?" yelled Paige.

"I don't know! Find it!" called Phyllis. She glanced up at Ashley. "You mean that country club party?"

"Yes," said Ashley.

"That party's on . . . New Year's Eve?" said Phyllis.

"Yes! You knew that!"

"Shhh! Maybe I did know. Let me think for once, will you, Ashley? Don't hound me. I've got more to worry about than the Ocean Crest Country Club. My gosh. Look at this Visa bill!"

"Mom!" called Paige.

Phyllis looked at the ceiling. "What!" she hollered back.

There was no answer.

"Ashley?" said Phyllis. "Keep this in mind: I don't keep your social events in my head. It's not my job. Did you mark this party on the calendar?"

"We don't have a year 2000 calendar."

"December thirty-first is not on a year 2000 calendar!" said Phyllis grumpily. "In the future, mark things on the calendar on the wall by the back door. Anyway, I forgot. And now I'm banking on you to hold down the fort on New Year's Eve."

"Hold down the fort?" said Ashley. "On New Year's Eve? Of the year 2000?"

"Yes. Flying out to see me is the first spontaneous thing Grammie's done in fifteen years. She's been so cooped up. Do you know that she couldn't even fly out for your father's and my *wedding*? I had to drag him all the way out to Florida to meet her."

"You mean when you and Dad went on your honeymoon and stopped off in Florida, on your way to Bermuda, and left me and the baby-sitter home to deal with the twins?"

Phyllis grew very quiet.

"When they were in their terrible twos?"

"They're still in their terrible twos . . . ," said Phyllis.

You can say that again, thought Ashley.

Phyllis looked down at her hands. "Grammie

wanted so much to come out here for your father's funeral. And that would have meant so much to me. But she just couldn't make it. She's had such a terrible fear of flying ever since . . . well. You know the story."

"Yes, I know the story."

"You're not the only orphan in town, Ashley."

"I know that, Phyllis. And I'm sorry about what happened to your parents. But—"

"I'll have you know," said Phyllis, "that Grammie hasn't even set eyes on my children. Except once, when I took the twins out to Orlando to visit her."

"You mean when you took the twins on a vacation to Disney World?" said Ashley. "And had your grandmother meet you guys there? And you all stayed in the Magic Castle, or whatever that place is, with five pools?"

"Yes."

"While I stayed home? And 'held down the fort,' with Dad?"

"Well, it wasn't your birthday, Ashley. And we couldn't *all* go . . . ," said Phyllis. "In any event, I would appreciate it very, *very* much if you would stay home with the girls on

10

New Year's Eve, so my grandmother and I can do something elegant. And memorable. And adult."

Ashley's heart began thumping. "But you said I could go to the party!"

"I'll duplicate everything to do with that ridiculous party, I promise you," said Phyllis. "You want me to pop a prime rib in the oven? You want Shirley Temples? And parfaits for dessert? Raspberries on vanilla ice cream! I'll get out the parfait glasses. Invite a friend over. Is Ana available?"

"No."

Phyllis wasn't listening. "And how about Emily? You'll be three peas in a pod. I'll buy you those little paper champagne bottle poppers, with streamers inside. You guys can rent movies to distract the twins. It'll be a blast! A real hoot!"

Ashley heaved a fat sigh. "It will *not* be a blast. Or a hoot! Nobody is available for Shirley Temples, peas in pods or prime rib! And even if they were, we hate big slabs of cow meat!"

"How about a small turkey, then?"

"I want to go to the party, Phyllis! This is not

just *any* party. It's the biggest party ever! With two thousand balloons!"

"Oh-kay," said Phyllis. "Oh-kay." She began slowly nodding and pacing. She suddenly whirled around. "You want balloons?" she asked Ashley. "I'll buy balloons. My friend Julia works at Spencer's Rentals and let me tell you, we can set you girls up with some major balloons, if that's what it takes to make you happy! Put in your order." She began rapidly clicking her fingers. "Come *on* . . . come *on* . . . how many do you want? You name the number!"

"That's *not* what it takes to make me happy!"

"Well, what does it take?"

Ashley stood her ground. "I want. To go. To the party!"

"I can't believe you're pressuring me like this," Phyllis muttered.

"Well, it's a very important party!"

"Oh, yes—I know," said Phyllis sarcastically. "I know all about it. Five families—the town royalty—make the Biggest, Most Very Important Party Ever for their five popular kids, and these five kids get together to determine who will be graced with an invitation . . . and therefore become officially certified as being in with the crowd."

Ashley blinked. What was that supposed to mean?

"And you're *totally down* for this whole event, even though your own best friends have been excluded. Am I right?"

Ashley didn't answer.

"Or wrong."

Ashley still said nothing.

"I thought so."

"Ana and Emily have plans! Their families are spending the whole weekend at the beach. In that same cabin they once rented, and invited me to. Right on the beach—out on that sand spit. Remember?"

"How would I remember?" said Phyllis.

"They're going to watch fireworks go off over the ocean," said Ashley, "then stay up all night around a campfire and watch the sunrise."

"How would I remember?" asked Phyllis again. "Was I invited along? No. Were the twins? No. Anyway—you know what? Good for them, for renting the cabin on the beach. I wish I had thought of something so good. I don't approve of this country club affair. And I *don't care* for the snob factor."

Stay calm, Ashley told herself. Stay calm and

say nothing until you think of something good to say.

"Well," she ventured a moment later, "just out of curiosity, Phyllis, where would you two go on New Year's Eve, with your bottle of champagne?"

"I haven't decided. This has all come up so suddenly—maybe the Shangri-La Room, at the Crown Hotel. I'll call and see what's shakin'."

What's shakin'—at the Shangri-La Room? thought Ashley. "Well, wouldn't it be better to drink champagne at home?" she asked, in as polite a way as possible under the circumstances. She didn't wait for an answer. "And do you *really* think it would be good to keep your elderly grandmother up till midnight—at *her* age?"

Phyllis closed her eyes and shook her head. "I'm a widow and a single parent, therefore I'm incapable of having a good time. Ha! Is that what you think, Ashley?"

"No."

"Good. Because *that* would be a rather sexist notion, wouldn't you say? And that an elegant and educated senior woman would be too far

14

over the hill to stay up till midnight? Or responsibly drink a glass or two of champagne? We're not planning to get tiddly!"

"I didn't say you were!"

"I'm surprised at you, Ashley. I really am."

"I'm sorry, Phyllis," said Ashley in a quiet voice. "That's not what I meant."

She watched as Phyllis gathered and straightened the bills and put them into the bill basket. "And I don't need a new dress," Ashley added. "I have my little black dress and Ana says I look good in it."

Phyllis turned to Ashley. "Trevor Cranston is one of the five giving the party, isn't he?"

Ashley's heart skipped a beat. "Yes."

"Well, as you know, his mother—Mrs. Robert W. Cranston—has an office right down the hall from me. Which she occasionally comes to. When she's not playing golf."

Phyllis raised an eyebrow.

"But Mrs. Cranston hasn't bothered to share any of her grand New Millennium's Eve party plans with *me*—no wonder I forgot about it!"

"The details are secret!" said Ashley. "They want the guests to be surprised!"

"Oh, nonsense. She hasn't brought it up to me because she doesn't realize that my stepdaughter exists, let alone that she could make it onto her Extremely Popular son's guest list."

"Mom!" cried Paige.

"What!" shouted Phyllis.

The house was silent.

"My friend Lily says Mrs. Cranston is really nice," said Ashley. "Mrs. Cranston volunteers after school to teach French to the French club every Monday. Lily's in the French club."

"Do I know this Lily?"

"Not really. Her name is Lilian Parks—but she goes by Lily. Please don't call her Lilian if you meet her."

Phyllis rested her hand on her chest and said, "I wouldn't dream of it!"

"Well, she hates that name!"

"Fine," said Phyllis. "I'll call her Lila, and—"

"Lily!"

"—I'm delighted you're expanding your friendships at school," said Phyllis. "You, Ana and Emily have been stuck together like glue since you were three twerps. How many years has it been?"

"I haven't counted. But Phyllis?"

"What."

"You've already decided you can't stand Mrs. Cranston—and yet you hardly know her. You told me you think you might prejudge people."

"Well, I didn't expect you to throw it back in my face."

"Sorry," said Ashley. "But you also said you need to reach out more to other people."

"I don't like it when you challenge me like this," said Phyllis. "It's disrespectful."

Ashley looked at the floor.

"Reeee-mote, reeee-mote, reeee-mote!" barked Paige from the other room. Then Ashley heard her two stepsisters join in one resounding "Remote!"

Phyllis stood up and began searching among the couch cushions. "My grandmother overcomes her fear of flying and makes a spur-of-the-moment decision to come all the way out from Florida to see her only granddaughter..."

"I know, but—"

"But what? To tell you the truth, Ashley, Grammie has been quite helpful to me financially over the years. She hasn't had much—but she's always been willing to share. She asked me not to announce it, but last year she sent me a check to start a college fund for you. She said she'd add to it—when she could."

"She *did*?"

"Yes. I admit that I had to dip into it for the twins' braces . . . but it was a thoughtful gesture on her part, Ashley. It goes to show she's thinking of you."

Ashley looked at Phyllis with an alarmed expression. "You spent all my college money on braces for the twins?"

"Well, not *all* of it went to the braces," said Phyllis, remembering. "A couple of hundred went toward the couch."

Ashley's heart sank. "Really?"

"Well, you *sit* on it, don't you?"

"Yes, but—"

"And you're planning to *sleep* on it, aren't you?"

Phyllis sighed very, very deeply and looked dolefully at Ashley. "Ashley?"

"What, Phyllis."

"Look at me."

"I am looking at you!"

"Really look at me—look deeply into my

19

eyes. I'm going to tell you something, in case you haven't already noticed."

"What is it, Phyllis."

"The twins weren't born with your God-given beauty. With looks like that, you won't need to go to college! *Comprendo?*"

Huh?

"Why the puzzled expression?" said Phyllis. "Okay—I'll say it in plain English: With looks like yours, you won't have to be bothered with a career. You'll marry well. You've got a regal look about you."

I *do?* thought Ashley.

"—with that long, queenly neck," said Phyllis, "and those slender, graceful fingers and toes, not peasant toes like mine and the girls'."

Ashley looked down at her feet.

"Your aristocratic cheekbones," said Phyllis, "and large, dark eyes, your perfectly arched eyebrows . . . these things run in *your* gene pool, Ashley, not *mine.*"

Ashley frowned.

"And I also must tell you, you have a pouty mouth. Models have to work on that look, Ashley—but you've come upon it, well, naturally."

Pouty mouth? That was the last kind of mouth Ashley wanted!

"To top it off, you've got a 'Draw Me'-style nose, the world's most perfect nose."

Oh, puh-leeze! thought Ashley. Now I've heard everything.

"The twins need to make the absolute most of their assets," Phyllis whispered. "You could have gotten away with a few crooked teeth; they can't. It's as simple as that."

For some reason, this conversation was making Ashley feel guilty.

Plus, she didn't agree with what Phyllis was implying about the future. Ashley had every intention of going to college, whether or not she had royally arched eyebrows or a college fund. She had twenty dollars in her Pooh bank. Plus her lucky fifty-cent piece.

Twenty dollars and fifty cents. That was a reasonable start.

For a fourteen-year-old.

And she didn't agree with what Phyllis was saying about her stepsisters, either. "I think the twins look fine," she said. "They *look* good, Phyllis—it's just that they *act* bad."

"Well, you're kind to say that."

I *am*? thought Ashley.

"*Anyway*," said Phyllis, "may I continue about Grammie? For a seventy-five-year-old formerly flight-phobic woman, a cross-country flight is a pilgrimage, not a plane trip. It might be the last New Year's Eve she ever celebrates. I know that; she knows that." Phyllis paused. Her chin began to tremble. "That's why she's coming."

Oops! Here goes the chin, thought Ashley.

"I'm happy she's coming," she told Phyllis. "For her—and for you. But I'm only asking—couldn't *somebody else* hang out with Paige and Jessica on New Year's Eve? Couldn't you hire a baby-sitter?"

"For *those two*? On almost no notice, on the eve of the twenty-first century?"

Think fast, Ashley told herself. "Well, why would they need a baby-sitter?" she said suddenly. "They're almost twelve!"

"Did I leave you alone when you were almost twelve?"

"I don't remember."

"Well, if I did, it was only because you've always been very mature, very dependable. They're not."

"Can't they spend the night at a friend's house?"

"They don't have any friends," whispered Ashley's stepmom. "Do they?"

Ashley shrugged.

"You don't think they could tag along with the Ana and Emily group, do you?" said Phyllis.

"Tag along, uninvited, for a *whole weekend*? Oh, right!"

"Well. It was just an idea." Phyllis shook her head. "I'm afraid the world is not ready for such assertive girls," she muttered.

Gosh, thought Ashley. You can say that again.

"Actually, even I am not ready for them!" added Phyllis with a smirk. "Oh, I know I've empowered them, I admit it." She began walking stiffly, like Frankenstein's creature. "I've created a monster!" She slowly raised her arms, with her hands outstretched and her fingers spread like claws. "In fact, I have created . . . *two* monsters!"

She made a scary face at Ashley, who frowned.

Then, "Coming, dumplings!" Phyllis sang

out, as if she and Ashley were sharing a joke. She dug deeper into the guts of the couch and yanked out the remote. *"Voilà!"* she said, waving it in Ashley's direction. "You think I can't speak French?"

Ashley didn't answer. Tears had sprung into her eyes, and they were just about to spill over.

"Oh, come on, Ashley—all is not lost," said Phyllis. "It's just that I wish you had reminded me—that you had somehow made me aware of how much this party meant to you."

Ashley blotted her tears with her sleeve. "How could you not be aware of that? The whole town's been talking about it."

"We'll work something out," Phyllis said sincerely. "We always do. Don't we?"

Ashley shrugged. "I guess so."

"But no matter what, Ashley, there is one promise I want you to make: If things don't work out, and you do have to stay home with the twins, you won't let on to Grammie that you're disappointed. I don't want her to feel like her trip out here is an imposition in any way— or that it got in the way of your doing what *you* wanted. Agreed?"

Ashley hesitated.

"But do remember—I *did* say, and let me repeat it," said Phyllis, "I'll think of something. I'll give it my best shot. In fact, I already have an idea."

"You do? What is it?"

"Ashley? Don't ask. I'm the parent, you're the kid. I'm in charge here. Okay?"

There was a thump, followed by a loud shriek. "Brats!" Phyllis mouthed over her shoulder as she headed out of the room.

Three

They would work it out somehow. Phyllis had an idea. Ashley hoped it was a good one!

She couldn't miss the party, she just couldn't!

Calm down, she told herself. You won't miss the party. Have faith!

In what? she thought.

She covered herself with the throw and tipped back the La-Z-Boy. She looked up at the light fixture on the ceiling, which was faintly illuminating a few delicate cobwebs.

Two of the three bulbs were burned out.

Ashley closed her eyes. She could smell the stale scent of Christmas tree. The house was quiet, except for the sounds of a distant conversation broken occasionally by dreadful organ music.

Good.

The twins were temporarily subdued by the soaps.

It was good to lie back and recuperate for a while. Just hearing Phyllis say "Trevor Cranston" had been enough to send a shock wave through Ashley's body.

Look, she told herself. There is just no way Phyllis can know that Trevor Cranston is the love of your life. You've given no clue. No signal.

And this was true. It was a secret locked tightly in Ashley's diary, and the key was around her neck, not far from her heart.

Only three people on earth knew this secret: Ashley, Ana and Emily.

And one frog.

Ashley would have enjoyed having Froggy on her lap right then, but she was too lazy to get up and get him. Hence the term La-Z-Boy, she guessed.

Ashley yawned.

Her thoughts drifted to Trevor.

The reality of her last encounter with him had been so stunning and amazing, Ashley had re-created it in her mind hundreds of times over the vacation. And she would now re-create it once again.

Start to finish ...

It was December sixteenth.

Ashley's drama class was rehearsing a play called *Royal Nonsense*.

Trevor was the prince.

Ashley was the narrator.

But during the rehearsal, the princess playing opposite Trevor, the lovely Kesha Hill, had to leave early for an orthodontist's appointment.

And a miracle happened: The director asked if the narrator could please stand in—and read Kesha's lines.

Oh yeah.

The narrator could most definitely do that.

Ashley could barely believe her good fortune: Not only did she get to stand close to Trevor and speak to him in a play where he loved her desperately, *the scene required her to faint and fall backward into the prince's arms.*

"Now, Ashley, you're frightened, shocked

actually," the director had told her, tapping on the script. "So you've got to react. Lose your balance, wilt and fall backward. The prince will catch you."

Trevor would catch her!

Ashley had to call forth all her acting skills to appear calm and focused on the director's directions.

"In a moment's time," he said, "you'll recover. You'll stir in his arms, open your eyes. Where are you? You don't quite know. You rest in his arms for a moment."

Oh-kay. *This* the narrator can do, Ashley had thought.

She'd looked over her shoulder at Trevor.

And even three weeks later, sitting here in the orange La-Z-Boy, she could make a perfect picture of his face in her mind: He had smiled, very slightly. Then he'd looked straight into Ashley's eyes and said, "Don't worry, I won't drop you."

"Trust him," the director had told her.

A moment later, she was waking up in Trevor's arms.

Darn it!

Why hadn't she taken longer to recover!

She was supposed to rest a minute before getting onto her feet again. The director had said!

In any event, just a few days after this fainting episode, an invitation to the New Millennium's Eve party at Ocean Crest Country Club had arrived at Ashley's house, completely unexpected.

Had Trevor been the one to put her name on the guest list?

If not, who had? Ashley barely knew the other kids hosting the party.

She sighed.

Mmmmmm-mmmmm.

The very idea that Trevor Cranston might have added her name to the list was almost more than Ashley could stand. It was a thought so breathtaking that she had mentioned it to nobody.

Well, nobody except Ana and Emily. But certainly not to Lily Parks when Lily had called her.

Obviously, someone had told Lily that Ashley was invited to the party, but Lily hadn't said who. And Ashley hadn't been able to think of a polite way to ask, so she'd just let it go.

Lily had called a couple of times over the vacation, to make sure Ashley was coming. Like Ashley would somehow change her mind?

I don't think so, thought Ashley.

Lily also wanted to fill Ashley in on what party information she'd wheedled out of Brittany and Mara, which wasn't that much.

But this was confirmed: The five kids hosting had made their list early, as early as October. Over the weeks that followed, there had been additions and deletions. Lily had no idea who had been bumped, or who'd been added.

But she did know that the list had been finalized by the first week in December and the kids had met just before the holidays to address the envelopes. The mailing of the invitations was timed so that they would arrive just after school had been dismissed for the holidays. That way, the guest list wouldn't be discussed at school; it would be easier on everybody. Fewer feelings would be hurt.

Even though Ana's feelings were very hurt.

And so were Emily's.

Ashley tried to picture the envelope-addressing event in her mind: Trevor, Brittany, Mara, Olivia and Evan, all seated in the living room of Brittany's undoubtedly very great house.

Maybe a fire was crackling in a fireplace with a mantel above it. Maybe there were pictures of Brittany's family members in silver frames lined up along the mantel. A beautiful, plush antique Oriental rug was probably on the floor, the polished hardwood floor.

There were possibly white couches with puffy white cushions arranged in a square in front of the fireplace, with a glass coffee table in front of them, and quite probably a large cut-glass dish full of nuts was in the middle of the table. Shelled walnuts, or possibly toasted almonds.

Or there might have been a jar full of candy shaped like Christmas ribbons on the coffee table, unless Brittany celebrated Hanukkah.

In which case the candy probably wouldn't have a Christmas theme.

But there still would be candy!

Was Trevor sitting close to any of the three girls?

Ashley hoped not.

She pictured a less cozy scene: Trevor and Evan were on one couch and the three girls were on the other.

Ashley heard a suspicious thud coming from

the direction of her bedroom. She booted the La-Z-Boy's footrest and brought the chair upright.

Where was Phyllis?

"Phyllis?" she called.

"In here!"

Ashley hurried into her bedroom.

"You're too much, kiddo!" Phyllis said with a chuckle. Phyllis was leaning against Ashley's desk, one foot crossed over the other, reading an essay in Ashley's English notebook. "I moved a few things so Grammie can make herself at home. I was ver-ry careful, *let* me tell you."

All the surfaces in Ashley's room had been cleared of knickknacks and other treasures. There was now a round lacy doily on top of her chest of drawers.

On it was a huge photograph, displayed in a brown cardboard frame, decorated with a golden art deco motif. "Wasn't she lovely?" Phyllis asked.

"Where's all my stuff?" said Ashley. She instinctively reached up and felt for her diary key, which was hanging from her locket chain, around her neck. "Where's my diary?"

"Oh, it's in a cardboard box, on the floor of your closet. You didn't answer: Was my grammie a splendid-looking woman when she was young? Or wasn't she. Look at those eyes!"

"Where's my green frog?"

"Maybe I take back what I said about my gene pool. Now, *that's* one beautiful lady," said Phyllis. "Your frog?"

"Yes! Where's my Froggy!"

"Look at those eyelashes! Would you? And she crocheted that lacy doily, I hope you know."

Ashley began frantically searching the room.

"Ribit!" said Phyllis, deep in her throat. She cupped her hand behind her ear. "Shhh! Can you hear him? Ribit," she croaked again. "Calm down," she told Ashley. "The frog's right here." She pulled open Ashley's underwear drawer. Froggy was stuffed in between some underpants, lying on his back, with one leg bent backward and trapped underneath him.

Ashley hurried over and took him out. She held him against her chest and patted his head. "He doesn't like being closed up in places."

"Sorry," said Phyllis. "And Ashley?"

"Yes?"

"Since you're being such a peach about giving up your room, I've decided that yes, we can

34

go on a shop-shop, just the two of us, while the girls are at ballet this evening. You were right about the sale at Starr's. And, party or no party, a girl can always use a new dress. Right?"

Ashley's heart sank. "I thought you said you'd figure it out so I could go to the party for sure!"

"But I didn't *promise*, did I?" said Phyllis.

Ashley didn't answer.

"Did I?" said Phyllis.

"I guess not," said Ashley.

"Anyway, I'll try to work my magic tomorrow. While I'm at the office, will you wash and change your sheets for Grammie? Strip the bed first thing when you get up."

"Okay," said Ashley.

"And Ashley? I hate to ask, but can you shovel the ashes out of the fireplace and give it a sweep? They've been there since Christmas Eve. Just dump them in the outside can. The trashman is coming before noon, so don't put it off, please."

"I won't," said Ashley.

"You're a muffin! Thank you. And oh, wow." What now.

"I forgot—the barbecue's a mess. And I'm planning to pick up a few oysters to barbecue for Grammie. She likes barbecued oysters with lemon. And Tapatío sauce. Can you imagine such a thing? Hot sauce? For a woman her age? And remind me," Phyllis mumbled. "I have some prune juice in the cupboard. I suppose I should chill it."

Phyllis walked out of the room.

Ashley sat on the edge of her bed. She looked at the picture of Grammie when Grammie was young. Phyllis was right, she was very splendid, with her beautiful brown eyes, full lips and close-cut cap of shining curls.

Ashley walked over and put Froggy next to the photo. She opened her closet door. In a box on the floor was a jumble of objects: her diary, which Phyllis had given her for Christmas, a tiny ceramic jar with Piglet dancing on the lid, a yellow plastic Pooh bank that she'd had since kindergarten, an assortment of hair clips—and an old blue autograph book with a picture of Curious George on the front. Had Ashley left her autograph book unzipped?

She couldn't remember.

Or had Phyllis gotten a little too curious, as she so often did?

Ashley picked up the autograph book and leafed through it. She came to the page Ana had signed in the fourth grade. On it, in rookie cursive and ballpoint pen, was written: "The rose of the valley may wither, the pleasures of youth pass away. But friendship will blossom forever, while all other flowers decay."

A wave of guilt slowly washed over Ashley.

Phyllis was right.

She shouldn't go to a party that excluded her two best friends. She, Ana and Emily had always stuck together. These friendships were the constants in Ashley's life. Ana and Emily had been there for her when her mother had died, when Ashley was in preschool. They'd been there when her father had married Phyllis, two years later. They'd been there, waiting for Ashley in the waiting room of the hospital, on the evening her father had died. And they'd been there at his memorial.

Don't think of that! Ashley reminded herself. Don't think sad thoughts!

Think of the future.

Of the new millennium.

The guilty feeling tugged and tugged at her. Yes.

Ashley should be spending New Millennium's Eve with her two best buds. But not firing off little paper champagne bottles full of streamers and batting around balloons. She should be sitting around a crackling campfire on the beach, outside the cabin on the sand spit. With fireworks exploding in the sky above. And waves breaking on the shore.

Not hanging around with a bunch of trendy kids.

Ashley found her party invitation at the bottom of the cardboard box. She looked again at the front of the envelope: This was definitely boy writing.

No doubt about it. The letters were crooked, and somebody had pressed too hard with the pen.

Ashley slid the invitation out of the envelope. On the front was a group photo of Trevor and the other four kids, all sitting on carpeted stairs. There was a tiny smudge of pink lipstick on Trevor's face, where Ashley had kissed the picture.

The phone rang twice in the kitchen and then was silent.

A moment later, Jessica barged in. "Oh. You're home?"

Ashley quickly stuffed the invitation back into the envelope and buried the envelope in the bottom of the box. She shut the closet door and leaned her back up against it. "Eeee-yeah. I'm home. Where else would I be?"

"The phone was for you," said Jessica. "It was Lily. Lily Barks."

Ashley stared at Jessica.

"Lily Barks." Jessica woofed. She began panting, with her tongue hanging out.

"Parks! It's Lily Parks! And why didn't you get me?"

"It's Barks! Lily Barks! And why didn't you get me?"

"I mean it! This isn't funny!" said Ashley.

"I mean it. This isn't funny!"

"What if I didn't know her number? Did you write it down?"

"What if I didn't know her number? Did you write it down?"

"I'd better be able to find that telephone number."

"I'd better be able to find that telephone number." Jessica flipped a piece of paper in the air over her head and walked out of the room, laughing.

Ashley quickly picked it up. She hurried into the kitchen and dialed Lily's number.

"Hello?" said a friendly voice on the other end.

"It's me," said Ashley.

"Oh. Ashley?"

"Yes?"

"Cool! Some girl said you weren't home. And, like, hung up on me?"

"That would be my stepsister, Jessica."

"Oh-kay . . . Anyway, here's the sitch: Kyle, Trevor, Evan, Roland, Marshall and a couple other guys booked a limo to take to the party. There were supposed to be, like, seven or eight guys going in it, but now two bailed. They couldn't come up with the money. So they now want the limo to pick you and me up."

Wake up! You're dreaming! Ashley told herself.

"They *do*?"

"Yup. It's thirty-five bucks each."

"It *is*?"

"But that's for both ways. And it includes the tip."

"Oh."

"Are you in?"

Ashley gathered her thoughts.

"Or not. Because we're supposed to pay up front. And no changing our minds once we say yes. There's a dad behind this with a credit card and he told the boys they have to collect all the money in advance."

Ashley didn't know what to say. Where would she get thirty-five bucks? Her total savings was in her Pooh bank, ten two-dollar bills and a fifty-cent piece, now earmarked for college. Should she rifle it?

It had only been designated as a college account for two hours!

"Can I tell you tomorrow?"

"When he calls, I'll ask," said Lily mysteriously.

"When who calls?"

"And I'll call you back," said Lily. "I hope you can come!" she squeaked suddenly.

"Me too!" Ashley squeaked back.

And she really, really did wish she could go. Not only because she'd never been in a limo in her life. And not only because Trevor would be one of the boys in the limo.

Take a deep breath, Ashley told herself.

But for another critical reason: From the very moment that she had been invited, Ashley had been having deep feelings of anxiety about where she could have Phyllis drop her off.

Ashley had never been to the Ocean Crest Country Club and so didn't have a clue as to where she might be dropped off without being noticed.

It was bad enough risking being seen arriving in Phyllis's station wagon, but now, with the hole in the muffler, Ashley could also be *heard* arriving in this frightful and embarrassing vehicle.

"Ashley? Are you there?"

"Yes—sorry!" said Ashley.

"Listen to me," said Lily. "Are you listening?"

"Yes!"

"Okay. Read my mind."

Lily became totally quiet.

"You need to come with us in the limo," she faintly whispered.

Ashley wasn't in receptive mode; her head was elsewhere.

What about a limo full of cute boys pulling up to her house, a modest house, to say the least, that didn't have a great address and, worse yet, had tan gravel in the front instead of a lawn? And a "garden" of half or totally dead cactuses?

Ashley would have to think carefully about this.

There was no time to landscape the yard or paint the house even just the front of it.

She wasn't even sure if Goodwill would come by in time to pick up the pile of giveaway stuff Phyllis had cleaned out of the attic, bagged and left by the side of the garage—for two weeks.

Besides, how could Ashley get the money to Lily in advance?

Lily chatted in an excited way for a few minutes, with Ashley barely listening.

There was a click on the phone line.

"Well, I guess I've got another call!" Lily said suddenly. "Gotta go! Bye!"

Ashley hung up the phone on the wall and stood in the kitchen, working things through in her mind. She opened the cupboard and stared at a box of crackers.

It would be dark by the time the limo arrived at her home. If she turned off the porch light, the front yard would barely be visible.

She took the cracker box from the shelf and peered inside. It was empty. She tossed it out.

Or she could give her neighbor's address and

be waiting for the limo outside his house! Mr. Anderson had a pretty house and a velvety green lawn, rosebushes and a birdbath.

And maybe she could hide his two ceramic gnomes.

But where?

Maybe she could say she needed to borrow them. For a science project at school, during vacation! A scientific study of ceramic gnomes . . .

But.

How could two fat Munchkin-style clay gnomes relate to science?

They couldn't. Well, if not science, then how about art? In what way could those two horrid creatures relate to art? In no way! That's what way!

Paige and Jessica swaggered into the kitchen, arms slung around each other's waists.

"Who puts empty cracker boxes back in the cupboard?" Ashley asked them.

"I don't know, but who's *Kyle*?" Jessica slyly asked.

"And *Evan*?" said Paige. "And *Marshall*? And *Trevor*?"

Ashley lowered her eyelids to half-mast and stared at them.

"The phone was on speaker in Mom's room—we couldn't help but hear," said Jessica innocently. "And we're just wondering: Is this the same Trevor that's in your diary?"

In my diary? thought Ashley. She reached up and put her hand over her diary key and pressed it against her skin.

"My diary?"

Her heart was beating so irregularly she thought she might need to call 911 for herself.

"Well, Santa Claus gave all of us identical diaries," said Paige with a smirk.

"So they all have the same key!" said Jessica. She smiled in a stupid way. "And, oops! We got mixed up. And accidentally read yours!"

"Sor-ry!" Paige sang out. "Mom?" she yelled. "You're not *really* going to let Ashley spend thirty-five dollars to ride in a limo, are you?" She turned to Jessica and whispered: "One . . . two . . . three . . ."

In one huge voice they bellowed, "That's. Not. Fair!"

Phyllis filled the doorway. "Girls? Beat it."

She signaled Ashley to follow her into her room. "I'll deal with them later."

Ashley and Phyllis sat quietly on the side of Phyllis's bed. Phyllis yanked a tissue out of the box on her nightstand and handed it to Ashley, therapist style.

"Thanks." Ashley wiped her eyes and honked her nose. She dropped the tissue into the trash.

"I should have known better than to give you all the same diaries," said Phyllis. "It was my fault. They were 'buy two, get one free,' so I figured, why not get a couple for the twins and have yours thrown in free? I regret it. And I'm sorry, Ashley. I really am."

"*You're* sorry? Why should *you* be sorry?" said Ashley. "This wasn't your fault. You didn't tell them to *read* my diary!"

"No. And I didn't tell them to put you guys on speaker phone in my bedroom and listen to your conversation, but they did. What can I tell you! They're snoops! Maybe they'll have a future as private investigators. Anyway, let's talk. Let's put the diary incident behind us and move forward, to limos. Now."

Phyllis helped herself to Ashley's hand, held it and patted it. "Why a limo for thirty-five dollars each person? I have six seat belts in the station wagon. Why don't I ask Mrs. Cranston if I can do the favor of transporting the kids and save—how much? Three hundred dollars?"

46

"No!" whispered Ashley.

"Well, it's the least I could do. Isn't it? With all the expense the Cranstons are going to."

"No!"

"And really, Ash. A limo? For a bunch of kids? Everybody's going to the same place. What's the driver going to do? Drop everybody off and park in front and be paid to stand around in a uniform listening to the frogs croak till the party's over?"

"Yes!"

"Why didn't you kids just hire the limo to drive you *back* from the party! Arrange for a midnight pickup at the country club and—"

"Phyllis? The limo's been hired till dawn!"

"It has?"

"Yes. After dropping me and Lily off, some of the kids might go for a ride. And watch the sunrise someplace. Maybe from Sonoma Mountain."

"Out all night in a limo?"

"Yes, because Kyle's grandpa owns the limo company. The driver is going to be one of Kyle's aunts. So she's the chaperone!"

"And this family still wants the money in advance? *Why?* They don't trust you guys to pay?"

Ashley shrugged.

Phyllis made a huffing sound. "Well, you'd think they could bend the rules a little, and do a little better on the price. But let me finish. Hear me out, would you? I chauffeur one way in the Nomad, the aunt chauffeurs the other in the limo. How's about it? The Nomad's a classic, and boys love classic cars! I'm even game for jumping out and opening the doors for you guys if you want."

Yikes! What a thought!

"Please, Phyllis! Don't ask Mrs. Cranston anything."

"Why not, Ashley? I thought you thought that she and I should get acquainted, and you know what? Maybe you're right. Here she's having this swell party and invited my stepkid—"

"Phyllis?" whispered Ashley. "I'm begging you. Leave things the way they are."

A shadow appeared under the bedroom door.

"Get away from there, you spies!" Phyllis cried out. She growled like a mad dog. Ashley heard a scuttling sound, the kind two groundhogs might make, scurrying away.

"Ashley?"

"What."

Phyllis patted Ashley's knee. "Can I just tell you something?"

Here it comes, thought Ashley.

"I think it's cute that you have a boyfriend."

Ashley cringed. "Well, we're not going *out* or anything," she said.

Yet, she added to herself.

"Well, it's still cute."

"When's dinner ready?" Ashley asked, jumping to her feet.

"So," said Phyllis, "maybe, maybe, maybe I'll let go of the chauffeur idea, me driving, that is. You want to go in a limo with a boy who's sweet on you?"

Ashley winced.

"You want to ride around with your crush?"

My *crush*?

"I can't say as I blame you. I was once thirteen too, you know."

"I'm fourteen," said Ashley.

"Well, then," said Phyllis. "What about *this*?" She slowly stood up, stood right next to Ashley, rested her arm on Ashley's shoulder and looked sideways at her. She raised her eyebrows and lowered them a few times.

"Want to have the boys come in after the party, for parfaits?"

Four

During dinner Ashley had managed to get Phyllis into the I'll *Think* About It Mode, in regard to sharing the cost of the limo, although the twins had furiously argued against this, citing evidence of Phyllis's past acts of favoritism. Toward Ashley?

What a laugh.

Miraculously, Phyllis had just chewed and listened, responding in the way a counselor had once suggested. Ashley had also refused the bait. She had eaten, cleared her plate and Phyllis's plate, rinsed them both, and walked out the front door. She paused on the stoop. The air was fresh and cool.

Ashley hopped down the stairs. She folded

her hands inside her sweatshirt pouch and stood in the driveway.

With her belly full of pork chops, applesauce, mashed potatoes and gravy, and the twins out of sight and out of earshot and soon on their way to ballet class, the world seemed full of promise and possibilities.

Yup. If Phyllis would share the bill, the limo was in the bag.

Cool!

Thank you, Aunt Rose! she thought. And Grandpa and Nannie.

Ashley was eternally grateful for the twenty bucks in two-dollar bills, which they sent to her on holidays and birthdays, enclosed in a card from St. Louis, Missouri. It felt good to be remembered by her father's sister and parents on every important day of the year.

But Ashley was especially grateful to them at this moment, when the twenty dollars would be available to help fund transportation to and from the most significant evening of her life so far. But secretly, Ashley wished they would send money in a more mainstream form of cash, like four fives, two tens or one twenty.

Who in the world would voluntarily use two-dollar bills?

A jumping spider made a mad leap onto the toe of Ashley's sneaker. Then it flew off and raced into a crack in the cement. Ashley leaned down to look at it. It raised its two front legs in the air to threaten her. Gosh. Get a little more hyper!

Did Trevor have cracks on his driveway? With weeds growing in them? And spiders who could kick-box? She doubted it. Trevor's father was an orthodontist, which was distantly related to a dentist, and dentists automatically plastered holes and cracks in anything. Ashley was sure of it.

Ashley took a couple of steps back and gazed at her house. It had definitely gone downhill since her dad had died. The paint was peeling. Some shingles were missing. Weeds were growing in the gutter, and along the gutter Phyllis had strung some unstylish fat-bulbed colored lights—not worth turning on, in Ashley's opinion.

Especially now that Christmas had come and gone.

Ashley strolled across the yard, listening to the gravel crunch and grind under her sneakers. She stopped to frown at the garden. The last of the golden sunlight lingered in the cactuses and lit the prickles of the tallest cactus, which was leaning against the neighbor's fence.

She stood on tiptoes and looked into Mr. Anderson's front yard. He had just finished watering, and droplets were sparkling and glistening in the garden like dew.

Too bad the rosebushes weren't in bloom, so that Ashley's backdrop could include twinkling rose petals as the limo drove up. But so what. Mr. Anderson had done an excellent job of putting teeny white lights in his evergreen bush; he'd certainly leave them in place through New Year's Eve.

In front of a twinkling evergreen bush was a perfect spot to wait for a limo. And any girl would have been proud to pretend Mr. Anderson's yard and house were her own.

Very proud.

Except for two minor details.

Ashley evaluated their positions: One was standing close to the birdbath, hands in his pockets, with his mouth frozen in a dreadful whistling position and his cheeks puffed out. The other was lounging on a huge mushroom that had a red-and-white polka-dotted crown.

The worst feature: His round little gut was showing, complete with a dent for the navel.

There was no doubt about it: The gnomes were unacceptable.

The question was: How heavy were they? And where could Ashley stash them?

For just one evening.

Without that nice, old, dignified yet dapper and dashing Mr. Edward Anderson noticing.

Could she just be honest with him, and tell him the gnomes would be happier chillin' in the backyard, out of plain view?

No!

What right did she have to tell a kind neighbor and elder gentleman where to stash his gnomes!

There was a house for rent across the street, a very pretty two-story, storybook house, with green shutters and a white picket fence. And no gnomes. How about standing there?

In front of a FOR RENT sign? Ashley asked herself.

Have you lost your mind?

She heard her front door open and turned to see the twins scamper out the door like two bad fairies, in leotards, tights and ballet slippers.

Their hair had been styled exactly like Ashley's, complete with rhinestone clips and terry-cloth ponytail rings.

Phyllis followed them out onto the stoop.

"I get the front seat!" called Jessica.

"No!" shouted Paige.

"Yes, she called it," said Phyllis. She turned to Jessica. "This time you got it, girlfriend!" Phyllis put her hand up to give Jessica a high five.

But Jessica just looked at Phyllis's hand and left her hanging.

She danced down the stairs.

Paige shoved her way past Phyllis and cut Jessica off at the bottom step. She raced to the station wagon, jumped into the front seat, locked the door and started licking the window.

Ashley watched with disgust as Paige made cross-eyes at Jessica and then pressed her tongue, lips and nose flat against the glass.

She looked like a pig with a ponytail.

And rhinestone clips!

Exactly like Ashley's!

Those rotten copycatters!

Phyllis came down the stairs, swinging her orange woven purse by the handle. "I know. I know. But I told you, it was half off," she called to Ashley, as if this were an adequate explanation. "And it does match my shoes. You have to admit."

Ashley looked at Phyllis's feet and winced, not only at the shoes, but also at the ten bluish white piggies unseasonably poking out from under the patent leather and protruding over the front edges.

This was Northern California, in winter. Not Maui!

Ashley slid into the backseat and yanked her seat belt out of the seat back. She stared at Jessica for a long moment before ripping out her own ponytail holder and clips. She shook her hair loose. "Whose lipstick is that?"

Jessica didn't answer. She folded her hands in her lap and stared at them.

Phyllis started the car. "I said they could use a little of your lipstick and they had to put it back." She glanced at Paige. "Guys? Did you put it back?"

Paige nodded.

Phyllis made eye contact with Jessica in the rearview mirror. "We did!" cried Jessica. "And we remembered to put the cap back on."

"Did you remember to *wind it all the way down* first?" asked Ashley.

"I don't remember," said Jessica.

Ashley dogged her. "Is that my body glitter on your neck?"

Jessica shrugged.

Phyllis slowly backed out of the driveway. Blue smoke from the exhaust drifted past Ashley's window. "Have you done a smog check lately?"

"Not that lately," said Phyllis, and they rumbled down the road. "There are different emissions rules for classic cars. But you're right; it's pretty rough on the environment. My original dream was to restore this baby to showroom standards. Now I'd settle for a new exhaust system."

I wouldn't, thought Ashley. And great, just great. We roll into the mall parking lot in a Chevy Nomad badly in need of restoration, now legally belching toxic fumes. Next: My stepmother steps out of the car, in orange platform clogs that match her purse.

Ashley really had to pause to think whether or not it was worth going shopping with Phyllis, just to get a new dress.

What if Trevor was there!

Calm down, Ashley told herself. You're a good kid, and there's no reason to imagine the worst. Don't torture yourself! she said in her cheeriest inner voice. Take a deep breath. Why would Trevor Cranston be in Starr's dressy dress department?

Ashley breathed in slowly with her eyes closed.

She pictured herself as a little girl, walking hand in hand with her mom and dad. She was in the middle, swinging her feet up off the ground.

She slowly exhaled.

And deeply inhaled again.

She heard Jessica whisper, "Ashley's acting like a freak!"

Ashley could feel her stepsisters staring at her, but she kept her eyes closed and concentrated on her breathing.

She heard a small snort and some forced laughter. "Mommy!" cried Jessica. "At first I was fake laughing and then it turned real! Just like the Velveteen Bunny, Mommy!"

"Rabbit," said Phyllis.

Ashley turned her head to the left so that when she opened her eyes she'd be looking out the window. She looked out the window and tried to time her blinks so she would have her eyes shut as each telephone pole passed. Meanwhile, Jessica hummed and hummed, and tapped and tapped her feet to drive the occupants of the car bananas.

She thumped on the back of Paige's seat.

Then she hummed and whistled and bobbed her head and tapped her feet and thumped and drummed her fingers on the back of the seat.

She suddenly stopped.

"Oh, Trevor! Trevor!" Jessica whispered. "I love you so much!" She began making loud smacking sounds by passionately kissing the palm of her hand. "I love you, Trevor! I love you!"

Say nothing, Ashley told herself.

"Oh, Trevor!" whispered Paige, clutching at her heart. "Marry me, I beg of you!"

I hate you! thought Ashley.

"You girls," Phyllis muttered. "What a coupla dingbats." She rolled down her window and stuck her elbow out.

I hate you I hate you I hate you I hate you, Ashley chanted to herself.

They drove down the boulevard, past the coffee shop and the park.

I hate you, hate you, hate you, hate you.

In the distance, Ashley could see a group of kids waiting on the corner for the crosswalk sign to change.

Uh-oh.

Who were these kids?

The light turned yellow and Phyllis slowed.

Ashley quickly put her hood up and drew her head down inside the body of her sweatshirt. She slumped way, way down in the seat. Only the point of her sweatshirt hood was visible from the street.

She could feel the car slowing down to stop at the light.

It was dark and safe inside her sweatshirt. Her breath was warm against her nose and mouth. She looked at the soft black backing of the fabric. You're safe, so relax, she told herself.

She closed her eyes.

She heard her heart faintly beating.

"Hey!" called Phyllis. Ashley stopped breathing. "Isn't that *Byron*? It is! Hey, Byron!" Phyllis yelled, and fully blasted the horn.

This is not happening, Ashley told herself. My stepmother did *not* just yell and honk the horn.

She pictured the twins, silently gawking; they probably had their mouths open, displaying the festive holiday red-and-green rubber bands on their braces, with their tongues hanging out.

Then: "Sorry!" Ashley heard Phyllis shout, with a laugh. "I thought you were somebody else!"

After an eternity had passed, Ashley could feel the station wagon begin to move slowly through the intersection and down the street. She remained housed in her sweatshirt. Was any of her hair poking out?

Nobody can identify you by a few strands of hair! she told herself.

But deep in her heart, Ashley knew that her hair actually was an identifiable characteristic: It was a long, bushy bunch of ringlets. And there was the possibility that a fair-sized clump of curls might have been exploding out of the hole.

Ashley sat in misery. Finally the car came to a full and complete stop.

She heard the doors open and heard Phyllis say, "Wait right in front, at eight-thirty—right under the light, just by the door."

Ashley heard footsteps running away.

She popped her head out and straightened her hair.

"I'll shut them," she told Phyllis, who was grunting and straining as she tried to catch hold of the door handle on the front passenger side.

Ashley got out and closed the doors; then she hopped into the front seat and buckled her seat belt.

"I really wish you wouldn't honk the horn at kids from my school," she quietly told Phyllis as they headed to the mall.

"Sorry," said Phyllis. "But I thought that was Byron Rowell, from down the street."

"He moved two years ago."

"Oh," said Phyllis. "Sorry." Then she gasped. She glanced at Ashley. "Oh, no. Don't tell me! It wasn't *him*, was it?"

"Who?"

Phyllis gave Ashley a look.

Yikes!

Was Phyllis trying to smooth in with Ashley and get Ashley to divulge information about Trevor?

"No! I just don't like it when you call attention to us like that. It embarrasses me."

"I understand," said Phyllis gently. "I was thirteen once too, you know."

"Fourteen."

"Right. I was fourteen once. And as I said, I'm sorry."

"But let's not make an issue of it," added Phyllis. "We two have an hour and a half to spend together. Just the two of us. Just us girls, without the twins. Let's make it count."

Phyllis held her hand flat out on the seat beside her.

Reluctantly Ashley rested her hand on top.

A second later, they were holding hands.

Twilight had fallen; the streetlights were glowing. White icicle lights were strung from the rooflines of houses. After the first of the year, they'd be put away.

The first of the year. Of the year 2000. Who would Ashley be with as the second swept toward midnight?

She couldn't say for sure. But she hoped that, once again, she'd be in the arms of Prince Trevor. But this time not playing the part of narrator posing as princess. She would appear as Ashley Toral, playing herself: a fourteen-year-old girl on the threshold of the rest of her life, which would magically unfold in the twenty-first century.

But that was two nights from tonight.

And for the moment Ashley had to admit it: It felt good to be holding hands with her step-mom, even if they were traveling toward the mall in a wide-bodied yacht with blue smoke belching out of the stack.

Five

"Always park near a light," Phyllis told Ashley. She docked the station wagon, inching it forward until the chrome bumper bumped against the base of a tall streetlight.

Ashley would have preferred to take the slight risk of walking a few extra steps in the dark than to have showcased the Nomad, now spotlighted in an upside-down funnel of soft pink light. She distanced herself from the car as quickly as possible.

As far as Ashley was concerned, a 1956 Chevy *alone* would have been fair grounds for revoking her party invitation, without even considering Phyllis's ventilated orange shoes and scary bag to match.

Ashley tortured herself as she briskly walked toward Starr's: What if Trevor pulled into the lot with his handsome dad, in his silver Porsche Boxter, which Ashley supposed an orthodontist would have? It was a small world; Trevor showing up wasn't entirely outside the realm of possibility.

Leave me alone! Ashley cried out to herself.

What if they roared in, screeched on the brakes and skidded to a stop—into the slot beside the Nomad?

Stop it, I mean it, Ashley warned herself. There's nobody in this parking lot but us.

She glanced over her shoulder at Phyllis's feet.

Is it my fault that my stepmother displays her toes in December?

No!

So shut it up! Ashley growled to herself. You've got an hour and a half to shop. Try to relax and have a little fun for once; nobody cares about your stepmother's car or accessories.

Nobody!

Except you!

Phyllis knew the rules about hand-holding in public, but for safety's sake, Ashley kept her hands in her sweatshirt pouch and walked a few steps ahead of Phyllis as they crossed the parking lot toward Starr's entrance.

She took one hand out briefly, to swing open the huge glass door.

The Starr's equivalent of a junior department was to the left of the entrance. Phyllis saw the sale signs and headed to the back wall, where there was a rack marked 75% OFF.

Ashley stopped to look at a small mannequin, standing alone on a circular base. The mannequin was wearing a short dress, dark and skimpy. The dress was covered with thousands of the tiniest, twinkliest rhinestones Ashley had ever seen.

A small beaded evening bag was hanging over the mannequin's shoulder by a delicate woven cord.

An older woman, kneeling, was in the midst of dressing the mannequin, and she looked up at Ashley and smiled.

There was something familiar about this woman, but Ashley couldn't say what it was.

Ashley smiled back.

"Pretty, isn't it?" said the woman. She gently brushed a thread from the hem of the dress. The fabric winked and glimmered as it moved.

"*Really* pretty," Ashley answered.

The woman lifted the cardboard lid from a shoe box. She took out one tall, bare high-heel shoe, with a crisscross pattern of satin straps across the front, an open heel and an ankle strap.

Ashley watched as the woman slid the foot of the mannequin into the shoe.

"A perfect fit," she told Ashley. She carefully fastened the strap around the ankle.

Ashley stared at the other shoe, resting in a soft bed of white tissue paper. "Italian," said the woman. "As you can see by the price." She smiled and turned the box to display the sticker.

Yikes!

"And there's nothing to them but a few flimsy straps. Stunning, though, I must admit. Nobody can make shoes like the Italians." The woman took the shoe out of the box and stood it on her palm. "How would you like to teeter around on a heel like this?"

"Actually, I'd love to," said Ashley.

"You *would*?"

"Yes!"

"At age, what? Fifteen?"

What a compliment.

Ashley was probably the youngest kid in her class, and if not the youngest, then certainly the smallest.

"Not quite," she said. "I turned fourteen three months ago."

"Well, that explains it," said the woman.

"It's a seven," she told Ashley, peeking at the inside of the strap to confirm the size.

"My size exactly," said Ashley wistfully.

"Slip it on," said the woman.

Was she kidding?

She handed Ashley the shoe.

Ashley clamped down on the heel of her sneaker with the toe of her other sneaker and pulled her foot out. She sat down on the rug and took off her sock. *I've gone crazy,* she told herself.

She pointed her toes and carefully steered her foot between the straps.

I am not sitting here on the floor of Starr's trying this shoe on.

Ashley's pinky toe temporarily got snagged on the wrong side of a strap, but she freed it and held her foot in the air.

"They're *you,*" said the woman. "Don't you think?"

"And you'll navigate in them very well,

I'm sure," the woman told her. She put the tip of her tongue against the inside of her cheek to keep from smiling. "As long as you don't stand up, walk or dance with boys in them."

"Right. And I'm *so not* interested in doing any of those things," lied Ashley.

She gazed at her foot and at her slender toes.

Maybe Phyllis was right.

Ashley did have some queenly features.

"No fourteen-year-old American girl is going to let a small matter of a five-inch wobbly spike heel and a staggering price tag stand in the way of happiness and fashion," said the woman. "So you're set. Right?"

Wrong, thought Ashley.

Because I also need the purse and dress to make me happy and fashionable.

"Right," she told the woman. "Except, how much is the whole outfit?"

"I'm not sure . . . but the dress looks like it would fit you perfectly."

As a matter of fact, it would.

Even though Ashley was small and young, and had been a bit of a late bloomer—yes. She definitely had enough going on to fill it up, as long as she wore it after eating a generous dinner.

"Let's see," mumbled the woman. "Where's the tag? Ah! Here it is." She adjusted her glasses. "Ouch! she said, checking the price. "But let me figure it out. The shoes . . . the purse . . . the dress . . . and maybe some earrings and a necklace . . ." She pursed her lips and frowned as she calculated in her head. "Have you got a fairy godmother?"

Ashley shrugged. "Maybe."

"Because if you do, we can turn you into Cinderella for, say, two thousand. Including tax."

Ashley and the woman smiled at each other. The woman seemed so familiar . . . Ashley glanced at her plastic Starr's name tag. MRS. CELESTE POWERS was inscribed in it.

Did Ashley know her from someplace? Where?

"Ash-es! Hi-eee!" Ashley turned to see Brittany and Mara hurrying toward her.

Yikes! She quickly took off the shoe, pulled on her sock, stood up and jammed her foot into her sneaker.

"Hi-eee!" said Brittany. "What are you, like, doing?"

"Thank you very much for modeling it for me," the woman said, discreetly picking up the high-heel shoe and sliding it onto the mannequin's foot. "I hated to bother you by asking you to put it on—but I wasn't sure about it. Until I saw it on an actual foot. Thank you."

"No problem," said Ashley.

"She's a good sport!" the woman said behind her hand to Brittany and Mara. She turned her back and adjusted the height of the purse.

Gosh!

What a great cover-up!

"I can't believe this, we were just, like, talking about you one minute ago!" said Mara. She made her eyes huge. "Oh. My. Gosh," she said, looking at the dress on the mannequin. "That dress is soooooo cute. I *cannot believe* how cute that dress is!" she said, as if she were in pain. "And the shoes!" she moaned. "And the purse! I can't stand it!"

"Are you, like, shopping for a dress?" said Brittany. "Who are you with?"

"Nobody," said Ashley. "My stepmom's around here someplace." Out of the corner of her eye, she saw Phyllis holding up a frightful plaid dress and checking the tags. Just keep on hanger-banging through the sale rack, Ashley instructed Phyllis in her mind.

In the meantime, I'm sorry! I'll need to put a little space between us . . . but I won't be far.

She casually strolled toward the cosmetics counters with the two girls walking beside her. "You know who we just saw in Sunwear?" asked Mara, after giving her wrist a spritz of perfume from the sampler. "Trevor and Evan!"

Don't react, Ashley told herself.

"And Kyle was there too. You know Kyle, on the basketball team?"

Mara offered her wrist to Brittany and Ashley, and they both sniffed it. "It's Millennium—by GUESS?. Like it?"

"Mmmm-hmmm," said Ashley and Brittany at the same time.

The girls strolled past a case full of sparkling hair accessories. They stopped to look through the glass.

"There are little rhinestone dragonflies on them!" whispered Brittany. "Aren't they the cutest?"

They were the cutest!

"And the silver necklace, with a rhinestone dragonfly?" said Mara. "And earrings?"

"Actually, they're diamond chips," said a pretty young woman behind the counter. "It's a set. Would you like a closer look, girls?"

"Oh, no thanks," said Brittany.

The three girls hurried away.

"Somehow I'm just not in the market for a set of diamond dragonflies," whispered Mara. *"Anyway,"* she continued. "*As* it turns out, the boys all had gift certificates from Sunwear and they were trying to pick out new snowboarding beanies. All except for Evan. Anyway, it's like, Cute Guy Night at the mall or something!"

Brittany and Mara looked at each other.

Then suddenly Brittany took Ashley's elbow. "You cannot tell anybody," she said. "Promise?" She squeezed Ashley's arm. "Actually, first we saw the guys coming out of Felix's Formal Wear, near the Candy Jar. So we decided to run over and say what up? and they told us this, like, huge secret: They rented tuxes for the party! They had to go to Felix's to, um, check the fit? They pick them up tomorrow!"

"Isn't that the cutest thing? The boys! All dressed up, for once!" said Mara. "And they're, like, really into it! I mean, they were talkin' cummerbunds! Isn't that funny? But we didn't laugh. And we *promised* we wouldn't tell anybody, so don't, 'kay?"

"I won't," said Ashley.

"Kyle's and Evan's? They're white, with tails!" whispered Brittany. "I hope they took out tux insurance," she added. "In case one of the boys busts out a football at the party."

"That's exactly how my dad ruined his tuxedo!" said Mara. "Last year, at my aunt's wedding! My mom's still mad about it."

Suddenly Ashley heard Phyllis loudly shout her full name across the store. "Ashley! Ella! Tora! Where are you?"

Ashley froze.

"Ash-ley El-la!" Phyllis called. "Can you hear me?"

Brittany and Mara looked at each other. "Who is *that*?"

"Where *are* you!"

"That would be my stepmom," said Ashley apologetically.

"Your middle name is Ella?"

"Gotta go, see you guys," Ashley said.

Don't blush, she told herself as she hurried away.

She stormed up to Phyllis, who was now standing in the middle of Starr's, directly in front of the entrance, holding an armload of clothes. "Where *were* you?" cried Phyllis. "You scared me! Where did you go?"

"I don't want any new dresses. I just want to get out of here."

"But these are an additional ten percent off of seventy-five percent!"

"Phyllis? I want to leave," said Ashley. "I don't want any new dresses. I don't like you to shout my name in a store, either," she added bravely. "And I don't like to advertise my middle name."

Phyllis knew that!

"I don't like velvet dresses with bows in the back," continued Ashley. "I'm fourteen, Phyllis. Not five."

"We could take off the bow. See?" Phyllis burrowed into the inside of the dress and demonstrated to Ashley that the bow was just barely tacked on. "Just snip the thread and it's off completely."

Ashley crossed her arms on her chest and stared off into space, in the direction of the front doors. I'll just stand here and stare into space at nothing, she vowed to herself, until Phyllis hangs those dresses back up.

Ashley picked a point in the air halfway between where she was standing and the front doors of Starr's and gazed at it with a blank expression, just the way she'd told herself she would.

Until Trevor Cranston and Evan Moore came into focus.

"Please put the dresses back," Ashley whispered in a panic. "Please hang them up; I don't want any dresses. I like my little black dress."

Phyllis shrugged. "Okay. If you say so. But I'm telling you—these are an awfully good buy." Phyllis clip-clopped away, the inside of each shoe slapping the bottom of her foot with every step.

"Hey," said Trevor. "What's up?"

"What did you get?" Ashley asked him.

Was that a dumb question?

Trevor opened his Sunwear bag and pulled out a blue Burton beanie. He stuffed the bag against Evan's chest. Then he put on the beanie and turned up the edge. "What do you think?"

Ashley checked it out. She nodded, very minimally, as a sign of approval.

"Want to come snowboarding with us sometime?"

"I don't know how to snowboard."

"We'll teach you. Won't we, Evan?"

"Yup."

"Okay," said Ashley.

"Is she goofy or regular?" asked Evan.

What was that supposed to mean?

"Don't move," said Evan. He walked behind Ashley and gave her a gentle nudge in Trevor's direction. "Goofy," he decided when she stepped forward to catch herself.

Ashley was now practically standing nose-to-nose with Trevor. He glanced down at her foot, then back up into her eyes. "I'm regular. You coming with us in the limo?"

"I'm not sure yet," said Ashley.

"Yes, you are. We'll pick you up at seven-thirty."

"No, I'm really not. Anyway, you don't know my address."

"I don't?" said Trevor. He gazed into Ashley's eyes for a moment and smiled, ever so slightly. "Come on, Ashley . . . you've got to come with us."

Ashley blinked.

"I have to go now," she said.

"Wait. Page me later and I'll talk you into it: 555-0088."

"Fine."

Ashley hurried away. Where was Phyllis?

Five, five, five, zero, zero, eight, eight, Ashley told herself. But, how did a pager even *work*?

"Phyllis!" Ashley squeaked as soon as she saw her. "Can we stop by Sawyer's News on the way to get the twins?

"Five, five, five, zero, zero, eight, eight," Ashley whispered.

"What?"

"Sawyer's News. Can we go?"

"I suppose so. For what?"

"Do you know how to use a pager?"

"No. Who has a pager?"

"Actually, Trevor Cranston does."

Why did I tell her *that?* thought Ashley.

"He *does?*"

Change the subject! Ashley told herself.

"What time is it? Let's get out of here," she said. She linked her arm through Phyllis's and steered her out of the store, via the cafe. There was no chance of running into anybody under the age of seventy in the Starr's cafe, at least not on a weekday evening. Ashley was safe. She was so excited about the encounter with Trevor that she squeezed Phyllis's arm and then allowed herself to take the risk of snuggling the side of her face up against Phyllis's shoulder.

For just one second.

And in that one second, Ashley saw herself

wearing a white Burton beanie, a white snowboarding jacket and gray snowboarding pants with white piping. She was carrying a sky blue snowboard, with a frog on it, sitting on a lily pad next to a huge, pink flower in full bloom. With a dragonfly hovering above it, with transparent wings reflecting rainbow colors.

"Sawyer's News, for what?" Phyllis asked again.

"I need a snowboarding magazine," said Ashley. "I need to know why I'm goofy."

"Ah," said Phyllis.

"And not regular."

"I'd like to know that too," said Phyllis.

Ashley saw herself walking, now with Trevor beside her, matching her stride step for step. Trevor's dad had driven them up to Tahoe, just for the day.

Hmmmmm.

How could you fit two snowboards in a Porsche Boxter?

"Ashley?"

"Yes?"

"You need to promise me something," said Phyllis, and now her voice was crisp. "You will *not* ask to go snowboarding. Skiing, maybe. Snowboarding, never."

"Why!"

"And this is *not* a negotiable topic," Phyllis added with a frown. "I read an insurance report recently that said there may be as many as ten times more snowboarding injuries as skiing injuries. So. If you want a snowboarding magazine, fine. I'll spring for a snowboarding magazine at Sawyer's. Beyond that, the answer is no."

"But—"

"But nothing. The answer is no and I want to make sure you understand that right up front." Phyllis stopped walking. "I may not be able to pick out dresses that meet the standards of a spoiled fourteen-year-old who's too old for bows and too upscale for the seventy-five-percent-off rack."

Whoa! What a mood swing!

Defend yourself! Quick! Ashley told herself.

"I didn't say you—"

"You may feel that as a thirty-something woman," snapped Phyllis, "I'm no longer with it enough to find a place to celebrate a new millennium. Maybe I'm just an all-around dope from your viewpoint, I don't know. But when it comes to insurance matters, little lady . . ."

Phyllis pinched her lips closed very tightly,

so that her mouth became a thin slit across her face. She began slowly nodding her head up and down.

Up and down.

And staring at Ashley with an icy expression.

"When it *comes* to insurance matters . . . I *do* know what I'm talking about."

"Fine!" said Ashley. "I know you know about insurance."

"You embarrassed me in that store," said Phyllis in a sharp tone. "In fact, you embarrassed me to tears, practically. Do you think I should have to prove to you that a bow is removable?"

"No."

"Do I need to apologize because I buy my things on sale? That I know how to stretch a buck?"

"No!"

"You're turning into Quite the Little Snoot, after just one party invitation. And after your snootish antics in Starr's."

Snootish? thought Ashley.

"And your little sassy snip routine about those nice garments I found for you. And your lit-tle disappearing act, which scared me *half to death*. You petrified me back there!"

"Phyllis! I was fifty feet away, sniffing perfumes with a couple of friends."

"Don't talk back to me! You vanish from the face of the earth and scare the daylights out of me and then *you* glibly tell *me* not to call out *your* name. What's the matter with this picture, Ashley?"

Ashley shrugged. She didn't know what *glibly* meant; a shrug was the only safe response.

"Oh," said Phyllis sarcastically. "You don't know?"

Oops. Bad answer.

"Well. I. Don't. Know. Either," said Phyllis. "But I'm telling you, Ashley, I am now going to be thinking *long and hard* about spending my time working out a child care situation for the twins so that you can trot yourself off to a country club . . . and till one A.M., no less? And in a limousine?"

"I'm sorry! I should have told you I was going to look at hair clips with Brittany and Mara!"

"Who the heck are Brittany and Moira?"

"Mara!"

"A minute ago you said you were at the fragrance counter!"

"I was, but—"

"Now you say you were at hair clips! How will I know you'll stay at Ocean Crest Country Club and not go running off someplace with your friends? Your affluent friends?"

"I won't. I mean I *won't* go running off. I *will* stay where I belong!" said Ashley, now in a panic. "In the ballroom! I promise!"

"The ballroom? This club has a ballroom?"

Don't speak, Ashley told herself.

"Next thing I know," cried Phyllis, flinging her arms into the air, "you'll be wanting to 'weekend' in Tahoe!"

Ashley unscrewed the top of the tiny aluminum espresso pot, took out the perforated metal basket and dumped the grounds. She rinsed the pot, refilled it with water and carefully poured coffee beans into the grinder.

She gently closed the kitchen door, turning the knob to catch the latch. She wrapped a dishtowel around the grinder to muffle the sound of the motor. She pressed the button and the blades whirled around.

Ashley packed the basket with ground coffee, screwed the pot back together and set it on the stove. She ver-ry quietly lifted a bowl from the stack of bowls in the cupboard and shook some oat cereal into it.

She selected three good strawberries from a green plastic container on the counter. She pulled off the tops and rinsed the berries in a thin stream of water, then sliced them onto the oat cereal. She put the bowl of cereal, a spoon and a napkin on the kitchen table, on a clean, woven place mat.

She found Phyllis's tiny espresso cup and saucer and put them next to the napkin and spoon.

Ashley opened the back door a crack and peered outside. There was one yellow flower blooming on a bushy daisy plant at the edge of the brick patio in the backyard. She slowly swung the door open, just enough for her to slip outside. Above her the sky was pink; the air was clear and cold. She walked down three steps and stopped to stare at the barbecue. There was a perfect, cone-shaped mound of ashes on the tray beneath the grill; the grill was charcoal black and coated with grease and incinerated bits of old meat. Some distance away, lying upside down in the dirt between two scraggly bushes, was the black barbecue lid. Filled with icky water.

Oh, great. *Clean and wire-brush the barbecue* was on Ashley's list of chores for the day.

She hurried gingerly across the bricks, picked the daisy and tiptoed back up the stairs and inside the house, gently closing the door behind her. She put the daisy in a bud vase and put the bud vase on the table. She glanced at the clock. Then she hurried back into her room. She took the clear plastic cover off the top of her box of blank note cards, helped herself to a large card with daisies on the front and dug down to find an envelope.

She wrote in her best cursive,

Dear Phyllis,
I'm sorry about what happened at Starr's yesterday. Don't worry about anything. Like I promised, the chores will be done. The chicken and scrubbed potatoes will be in the oven by 4:30. The house will be perfect when you and your grandmother come home.

Hmmmmm. How should she sign it?

Regretfully, Ashley

Good.
Ashley licked and sealed the envelope,

kissed it for good luck and rested it against the bud vase on the kitchen table.

Then she climbed back into her bed and snuggled up with Froggy. She pulled the covers over her head, leaving a small space for fresh air to leak in. Once a prince, she thought, now a simple, formerly fluffy frog. Transformed from royalty to amphibian via fairy sparkles from a fairy's wand. From a magical fairy with transparent wings . . . like dragonfly wings . . . that shimmer like cellophane rainbows . . .

Save it, Ashley told herself.

But she really truly did love her Froggy; she'd had him since she was two. Her dad had made up the fairy dust and prince part. Her mom had chipped in the dragonfly wings.

Ashley yawned.

She snuggled deeper into her covers when she heard Phyllis's footsteps in the kitchen. It was dark and hot under the blankets. Ashley put her perfect "Draw Me" nose into the exact spot where fresh air was seeping in.

She heard the espresso pot gurgle and the refrigerator door open. She heard the clinking of spoon against cereal bowl. She heard a chair scrape across the linoleum, the front door open and shut.

Phyllis wasn't going to come in to say thank you?

After all that?

Ashley heard the car start and chug backward out of the driveway. And rumble away down the road.

Guess not . . .

She pulled Froggy closer so he was crammed right up against the buttons of her nightgown.

Gosh.

Phyllis didn't even come in to whisper thanks and say goodbye?

How could she still be mad?

A wave of emotion washed over Ashley; the day ahead seemed overwhelming. She had hours of chores ahead of her. Would Phyllis arrange for child care, as she'd practically promised?

She had to!

Or would she use Ashley's bad behavior at Starr's as an excuse to keep Ashley at home.

No! Nobody could be that mean, not even Phyllis, thought Ashley. Well, hopefully not Phyllis.

Ashley patted Froggy's back.

Froggy, she thought. At this moment, you are my only connection to my mom and dad. Everything else we shared is gone.

Gosh. What a crushing thought.

That's not true! Ashley told herself. There are lots of other things, like photographs. And all the books we read together, all the fairy tales!

Despite this courageous fight to hold the sadness back, a sad, sinking feeling crept into Ashley's heart.

Froggy, Ashley silently pleaded. Listen to me. If there's any magic left in the world, if there are any magic twinkles in the air, in or around your body, just grant me one wish.

Two huge tears ran down Ashley's cheeks and soaked into her pillowcase.

Please help me not to mess up anymore with Phyllis.

A little sob escaped from Ashley, and she covered her face with her hand and cried, with her shoulders shaking.

And don't let the twins ruin my chances of going to the party! she pleaded. Let Phyllis find someplace for them to go or someone else to stay with them besides me!

She sobbed and shook some more.

Then her breathing became steady again.

Ashley threw the blanket from her head. Get *over* it, she told herself. Quit being such a drama queen. And get real! Like a stuffed green frog is going to solve your problems?

Grow up!

Ashley sat up and wiped her nose on her nightgown sleeve.

She tucked Froggy in properly: on his back, with his back legs under the covers, his front legs over the covers and his head resting nicely on the pillow.

And his yellow glass eyeballs staring straight at the ceiling.

Get dressed, Ashley told herself. Clean the house. Think positive thoughts.

She walked across her rug and honked her nose on a tissue. Then she peered at her nose in the mirror on the closet door. You've got this perfect "Draw Me" nose. Right?

And what about this long, royal neck? She stretched her neck out and felt the soft skin on her throat. She raised and lowered her regal eyebrows at herself in the mirror. "See?" she whispered. "The queen ain't got nuthin' on you, girlfriend!"

I'm a jackass, Ashley admitted to herself.

She flung off her nightgown and got dressed in jeans, a T-shirt and black rubber flip-flops.

If I have royal blood, she asked herself, then why am I so short? Huh?

Huh?

Ever heard of a queen that was five one?

With her shoes on?

Who can't sleep away from a stuffed frog, at age fourteen? Who *talks* to a stuffed frog, at age fourteen?

Ashley stood poised in her bedroom doorway for a moment, with her nose in the air, before solemnly marching toward the utility closet. She opened the door and helped herself to the sheepskin duster.

She screwed the wooden extension onto it. This would take care of the cobwebs on the light fixture on the living room ceiling.

Were there any extra lightbulbs?

Yes.

She knocked a cardboard carton of bulbs down from the top shelf and caught it.

Holding the duster like a fluffy imperial staff, Ashley glided majestically through the kitchen, with her head high and one eyebrow cocked at a lofty angle. And the box of lightbulbs tucked under her arm. She eyeballed the table. Phyllis's dirty breakfast dishes were still on the place mat. The milk was out. The bud vase had tipped over and the daisy was lying on its side, gasping for water.

The envelope was torn open; apparently Phyllis had read Ashley's note. And . . . good heavens! Ashley's heart fluttered. What was this?

She put down the bulbs and duster.

In the envelope, Phyllis had tucked a ten . . . four ones . . . and two quarters! Cool!

Scrawled inside and on the back of the flowered card was a long note:

This is not, I repeat not, confirmation that you can go, but here's my part of the limo fee—since these people are demanding the money up front.

You can thank me by doing an extra good job on the house and by being extra patient with the twins. It's hard for them to have a working mom. Especially during their vacation. Like I told you, I'll see what I can put together for child care for them. No promises, though.

No matter what, remember that I don't want Grammie to sense any kind of disappointment on your part if I can't make arrangements for the twins. I don't want her to feel like she's imposing on you, me or any-body else, and I DO want her to have fun on New Year's Eve! See you tonight.

Phyllis

Ashley stuffed the money into her back pocket and tossed the note card into the trash. She refilled the bud vase and poked the daisy back into it. She brought it into her room and set it on her chest of drawers.

Too bad she had to spend her lucky fifty-cent piece, but oh, so what.

What could be luckier than a limo ride to a dance welcoming in the new millennium?

Working from the top to the bottom and saving the vacuuming for absolute last, Ashley cleaned the living room. She stood on a chair and replaced the lightbulbs. She dusted the blinds and the bookshelves and the top of the TV.

She took glass cleaner, scouring powder, toilet bowl cleaner, rubber gloves and a gray plastic bucket with a rag in it into the bathroom and closed the door—so she wouldn't disturb the twins.

She wiped a big, dumb smiley face off the mirror—drawn by one of the twins' grubby fingers.

She scrubbed the sink and tub with the scouring powder and rinsed them with warm water. She cleaned the back of the toilet, the metal flusher and the toilet seat with a rag. Then she carefully uncapped the bowl cleaner and squirted a blue line of disinfectant from the bottle under the rim of the toilet.

She heard a clink! sound, and then the pitter-patter of some fairly sizable stockinged feet.

Rats!

They were up.

Ashley scrubbed the bowl with the plastic toilet brush and flushed the water. Then she scrubbed and flushed again. She banged the handle of the brush against the enamel rim of the toilet to get rid of the drips. She was just replacing it in its plastic holder in the corner of the bathroom when there was a thunderous bang on the door.

"Let me in!"

"It's open."

In walked Paige, with one eye shut. "Why are you making so much noise flushing the toilet when we're trying to sleep?"

Ashley said nothing.

"Can you get out?" Paige asked her. "Shut

the door!" she bellowed just as Ashley was reaching for the door handle.

Ashley pulled the door closed and went into the kitchen. It was Jessica's turn for dishes, but the negotiations wouldn't have been worth the effort. Ashley washed Phyllis's breakfast dishes, put away the milk and shook out the place mat.

She wiped off the kitchen table, cleaned the top of the stove and was sponging the cupboards clean when she began to have the odd feeling that she was being watched.

Jessica peeked around the doorjamb. "Where's the gardening trowel?"

"I don't know. Why?"

"I've been looking out my bedroom window into the backyard and thinking I'd like to do some gardening today. Beginning with this." Jessica held up a small potted plant. "I need to plant my Venus flytrap out there. It's not a happy camper in my room."

No, thought Ashley. I'll say it's not. And neither would I be, if I lived in your room.

There was nothing left of the plant but a few floppy stems with shriveled tips.

"Have you tried talking to it?" said Ashley.

Jessica lifted the flowerpot close to her

mouth. "Grow!" she screamed at the plant, and Ashley jumped. "Right now!"

"Can you wipe off the refrigerator door for me?"

"No. Where's the trowel?"

"The trowel is near the watering can, on the patio."

"Oh."

"Want to clean the barbecue while you're out there?"

Jessica closed her eyelids.

"I didn't think so," said Ashley.

Jessica pulled a clean bowl out of the dish drainer and inspected it. She pointed to one tiny speck of dried cereal on the rim and handed it to Ashley, who set it near the sink.

Jessica selected another bowl and dumped cornflakes into it. Standing in front of the refrigerator, she uncapped the milk with one hand and poured it over the cereal. The bowl tipped as she shoved the milk jug back into the refrigerator, and milk dribbled onto the floor. "Don't worry. I'm cleaning it up. See?" Jessica smeared it around on the linoleum with the toe of her sock. Then she skated across the kitchen and dusted her cereal generously with sugar.

How come Jessica is being so cooperative this morning? Ashley wondered.

Enjoy it while it lasts, she told herself.

Jessica made sounds like a horse munching oats. "So anyway," she said as she shoveled another large, dripping spoonful of cornflakes into her mouth. "I'm going to do a little gardening this morning. Paige said she'd help me."

"She *did*?"

Ashley listened for Paige noises.

The house was awfully quiet.

"Where *is* Paige?"

Jessica shrugged.

"Leave me alone," Paige called from their bedroom. "I'm reading about . . . bears hibernating."

Ashley smiled to herself. Paige was in a good mood; she and Jessica would soon be out digging in the garden. Ashley's work was going well. All Ashley had left to do was wash the sheets and dry them and put them on her bed, clean the ashes out of the fireplace, vacuum the rugs, mop the bathroom floor and get dinner into the oven by four-thirty.

And wire-brush and scrub out the barbecue.

The phone rang and Ashley picked it up. "Hello?"

She heard the click of another receiver being lifted.

"Hey," said a boy's voice.

"Hey," said Ashley.

"Is this Ashley?"

"Mmmmm-hmmmm . . . Who *else* is on the line?" Ashley asked.

"You didn't page me," said Trevor. "So I had to get a friend to help hook me up with your number."

Ashley brought her hand up to her mouth.

Oh. Mygosh. Was this *Trevor?* Say something!

"What's up," she said.

"What's up is that this is a conference call," Trevor told her. "Since Lily wouldn't actually give me your number. Lily? Are you there?"

"Hi, Ashes!" said Lily.

"Hi, Lil!" said Ashley.

Both girls giggled.

"So, are you coming with us in the limo," said Trevor, "or not? And can Lily give me your number?"

Ashley heard whispering on the line, then distant, muffled belching noises. Then one loud and long Bronx cheer.

Those jerks!

"Just . . . a minute," she told Trevor and Lily, her voice trembling.

"Get off this line! Hang up! I'm sick of you two!" she shouted at Paige and Jessica. She pressed Flash to put Trevor and Lily on hold for a minute and stormed into Phyllis's room.

Jessica was lying facedown on the bed, pretending to be sleeping, with her eyes squeezed shut, her mouth fallen open, her tongue flopped out.

And she was snoring.

"Where's Paige? Under the bed?" Ashley lifted up Phyllis's bed skirt and looked under the bed for Paige. "I know both of you losers were on the line."

Ashley reached behind Phyllis's nightstand and jerked the plastic phone wire out of the jack. She yanked the plug of the answering machine out of the wall, picked up the cordless phone/answering machine from the nightstand and started to cart the whole contraption away. But she tripped over the phone cord and the receiver tumbled off its holder and clattered onto the floor, under Phyllis's dressing table.

Ashley got down on all fours and picked up

the skirt to look for it, thinking, Who in this day and age has a dressing table, with a skirt on it?

Who!

Jessica opened one eye and smiled as Ashley poked her head under and grabbed the receiver. A large clump of dust had attached itself to the antenna. Ashley pulled it off and it floated down to the carpet like a small gray cloud.

"Pick up that dust bunny!" Jessica told Ashley. "Or I'm telling my mom."

Ashley jammed the receiver under her armpit and scrambled out of the room, hugging the answering machine against her chest and trailing the wires behind her. She quickly dumped everything on the kitchen table and hurried to the wall phone.

She pressed Flash again.

"Hello?"

Nobody answered.

"Hello?"

Ashley rapidly clicked the button on the wall phone. "Hello?"

There wasn't even a dial tone.

No! Ashley cried out in her head. Say it isn't true!

She quickly gathered the stuff back up from the kitchen table and rushed back into Phyllis's room. She dumped the answering machine onto the floor next to Phyllis's bed and frantically found and clipped the end of the plastic phone line back into the square hole in the jack.

She pressed the On/Off button on the receiver. "Hello?" But the little green light didn't come on. She pressed it again, and the light still didn't come on!

She plugged the answering machine back in and tried again. "Hello?"

There was no answer.

"Hello?"

Jessica giggled into the pillow, then began to loudly snore again.

Ashley raced back into the kitchen so fast she needed help from the doorjamb to round the corner.

She picked up the receiver.

The phone was dead.

Ashley felt numb. She'd put Trevor and Lily on hold, and then somehow the phone had broken.

How could this happen?

How?

I despise you! she told the twins in her mind. I loathe, hate and despise you!

I despise, detest and abhor you!

Where was Paige hiding out?

She was the worst of the two!

And what could be wrong with the phone again?

Mr. Anderson had already been over to fix it once. What was his deal, anyway?

Ashley wished the guy would learn to fix telephones right instead of clipping rosebushes, watering lawns and creating environments for whistling gnomes.

And gnomes kickin' it on poison mushrooms!

Don't blame him, Ashley told herself. It isn't Mr. Anderson's fault! Mr. Anderson, the world's nicest, most helpful, most debonair and gentlemanish senior citizen on the block, or gentlemanly, or whatever it is. And you're going to stand here blaming *him*?

Place responsibility where it belongs! she lectured herself.

Face it.

You blew it, Ashley told herself. And she was filled with a tremendous, choking sense of sadness and frustration.

You let the twins get to you; you blew it. Ana and Emily told you: Don't let them get to you. And they got to you. As a result, there's no dial tone. The phone is broken, and you can't call Lily back.

Or page Trevor.

Not that you even know how to use a pager.

You dope.

Seven

After seeing Ashley full-on sobbing, with her head in her arms on the kitchen table, the twins really had seemed remorseful.

"We're sorry, Ashes," Jessica had told the top of Ashley's head. "We really are. But Mom *did* say to be patient with us today."

When had they read *that* note? Ashley had wondered. Had they gone through the trash in the kitchen?

Paige had reappeared from somewhere, possibly out from under a rock. "It's hard for us to have a working mom," she had explained while Jessica had softly patted Ashley's back. "We're bored and restless. That's why we listened in on the conversation between you and your boyfriend—I mean friend! Sorry!"

At this point Ashley had heard a suspicious squeak. Had it been a little squeal of laughter squelched by Paige? Or was there a rat loose in the kitchen?

Two rats, Ashley told herself.

"I don't think it was your fault that the phone broke again," Jessica had added in a sympathetic way. "And I'm *sure* my mom won't ask for her fourteen-fifty back if Mr. Anderson can't fix it and the telephone repair guy has to come."

"Captain Whiskers? He didn't really even *fix* anything last time," mumbled Paige. "He just fiddled around with the jack in Mom's room."

"Yeah," said Jessica. "The dial tone just magically came back on its own! And he tried to take credit for it. Like the guy could actually fix something."

Shut up! thought Ashley.

"If you want, we'll say *we* trashed the phone—I mean *broke* it! Talk to us! Please!" Jessica had pleaded.

But Ashley had remained seated with her forehead resting in the crook of her arm, dropping tears of rage and staring at the tabletop.

And saying nothing, until the twins gave up and left the room.

Ashley had continued to say nothing, which had a very positive and productive effect:

After watching some soaps in their bedroom, the twins had made themselves peanut butter and jelly sandwiches and put both jars away. They'd closed up the bread and fastened it with the little white twisty—and put the bread in the bread box on the kitchen counter.

They'd sat and eaten their sandwiches; apparently neither showed the other what she was chewing. There were no food fights. Nobody ended up with peanut butter up the nose. They'd cleared their plates, rinsed them and put them on the tile counter right next to the sink.

Jessica had silently walked past Ashley, carrying the Venus flytrap through the kitchen and out the back door, being careful not to spill potting soil on the floor.

Paige had followed without speaking, quietly closing the door behind them.

And Ashley hadn't heard a peep from either one since.

In the meantime, Ashley had stoically shoveled out and swept the fireplace and dumped the ashes into the outside cans. She'd stripped her bed, washed and dried the sheets and made the bed again, in between mopping and waxing the bathroom floor and vacuuming the entire house.

She was now cleaning out the refrigerator.

And humming the theme song from *Snow White and the Seven Dwarves.*

Which was odd. She'd never liked the song.

Did other fourteen-year-olds hum Disney tunes?

Ana probably did. Ashley would have to ask her.

There was a knock at the door. "Ashles?" said a familiar voice.

It was Ana's mother! She opened the front door and stuck her head in.

"Hi!" said Ashley. "What are you doing here?"

"Well—somebody called Ana, saying she was worried about you—she didn't say why . . . or rather, Ana didn't mention why to *me,* and Ana tried to call *you,* and she got busy signals, busy signals, busy signals, so we had the operator check and she said you have a phone off the hook—so you know us. We decided to drive over."

"A phone off the hook?"

Ana's mom turned and waved in Ana, who was waiting in their car. "Everything's fine!"

Ana jumped out and ran up the front steps.

"But Ashley?" said Ana's mom. "You should lock the front door when you're home alone. I'll check the phones."

"Thanks!" said Ashley.

Ana walked up very close to Ashley. "*What* is going on? Lily Parks called me, totally freaked out! I hardly know this girl! And she calls me and tells me you totally unloaded on her—and Trevor?"

"She *did*?"

"You didn't even tell me you and Trevor were talking!" griped Ana. "It's like, ever since you got the party invitation, everybody's moving in on my best friend."

"Sorry," said Ashley. "I was going to call you when I got home from shopping last night, but Phyllis said—"

"How come you yelled at Lily and Trevor to get off the phone?" asked Ana. "And then hung up on them? Can somebody fill me in on what's going on here?"

Ashley froze.

"That's what Lily said? That I yelled at

them?" said Ashley. "That I *hung up* on her . . . and Trevor?"

"Eeee-yeah . . . that's what she said."

"But I didn't!" cried Ashley. "I said, 'Just a minute,' and put them on hold!"

"She said you yelled, 'Get off this line! I'm sick of you two!' " said Ana.

"That's what I yelled at Jessica and Paige," said Ashley, now totally distressed. "They were on the line, listening in, and making gross noises, in Phyllis's room!"

"Well," said Ana. "That's not what Trevor and Lily thought happened."

Ashley tried desperately to clarify the situation. "I put Trevor and Lily on hold and—"

"Whatever, Ashles. I'm just trying to tell you what Lily thinks," said Ana gently. "She thinks you're mad at her and Trevor about—"

"About the conference call?"

"Mmm-hmmm. I guess she and Trevor decided maybe you're not supposed to get calls from boys."

Oh, great.

Ohboy.

"Can you call her back for me and say what happened?" said Ashley. "Can you ask her to page Trevor? Or somehow get Trevor to call you?"

"The boy has a *pager*?"

"Yup—and he asked me to page him last night. But Phyllis got mad at me at Starr's and wouldn't let me use the phone."

Ana frowned. She made a little *Uh!* noise. "That's *so* unfair!"

"Otherwise I would have called you to tell you—I saw Trevor at the mall!" squealed Ashley. "And he invited me snowboarding!" She lowered her voice. "I was thinking of paging him behind Phyllis's back."

"You *were*?"

"But I don't know how to use a pager."

"Neither do I."

Ashley and Ana suddenly threw their arms around each other. "We don't know anything, do we!" cried Ashley.

"No!" said Ana.

"But you have to learn. You have to fix this for me," Ashley whispered. "You have to, Ana—I mean it. Talk to Trevor!"

Ana squeezed Ashley really tight. "I'll try."

"You're the only real sister I've ever had," whispered Ashley. "You and Emily."

"I know—me too," said Ana.

They squeezed and squeezed each other. "I wish I was going to the beach with you guys," said Ashley.

"Well, you're invited, you know that," said Ana.

"We should be spending New Year's Eve together," said Ashley. "You and me and Emily, watching fireworks over the ocean. And staying up all night, and watching the moon rise, and the sun rise. I want to be snuggled under blankets and make S'mores with you guys, around a campfire in the sand on the beach outside your cabin. Remember Campfire Girls?"

"We hated Campfire Girls!" said Ana.

"I'm already sick of the party," said Ashley. "I don't belong there."

"Yes, you do."

"No, I don't."

Ana's mom came back into the living room. "You're right—no phone off the hook. Do you just have the two? In the kitchen and Phyllis's room?"

"Yup."

Ana's mom looked thoughtful. "Where are the twins?"

"Gardening in the back."

"Ah," said Ana's mom. "Well, are you three okay here, without a phone?"

"We're fine. Mr. Anderson's home next door," said Ashley.

"Because I can leave my cell phone if you need it," said Ana's mom. "And pick it up later."

"Mom?" said Ana. "She said she doesn't need it."

"But thank you!" said Ashley.

"Okay then," said Ana's mom. "Well, if I don't see you—happy new year!" They hugged. "We'll see you in the next millennium!"

Ashley stood in the doorway and watched Ana and her mother go down the steps and get into the car. She waved as they backed out of the driveway.

Get back to work, Ashley told herself. Ana can help you work this out . . . have faith!

In what?

Don't ask! she told herself.

In the crisper drawer, Ashley discovered a medley of uncrisp organic objects, including three tomatoes that instantly assumed the shape of the bag when she picked it up and dropped it into the trash.

Behind a large, unopened bottle of prune juice, she found two frightening Tupperware containers, half filled with unidentifiable leftovers that had transformed themselves into greenish fuzz.

She cleaned out the containers and washed them.

Then she opened the freezer door and cautiously peered in. It looked like fresh snow had fallen on a stack of three "It's Amore!" individual pizza boxes that were poised and ready to tumble out.

She closed the door again.

Ashley glanced at the clock: It was 4:15 and time to take on the Salmonella Challenge.

Ashley carefully followed Phyllis's instructions on how to deal with a raw chicken—containing a small, wet paper sack filled with unmentionable body parts.

Ashley turned her head and looked in another direction as she held the chicken under the faucet and rinsed it—inside and out. Gripping the cold flesh, she tipped it upside down. At least a quart of pink water glugged out of the cavity and down the drain.

Sick!

She slapped the chicken body onto a raised rack in the bottom of a baking pan.

As per Phyllis's written instructions, Ashley

drizzled olive oil on top and "floated" a small piece of foil "over the bird."

Ashley then scrubbed five potatoes with the vegetable brush, stabbed them viciously with a fork, swung down the oven door and rolled them onto the rack. She shoved in the chicken and turned the temperature knob to 375 degrees.

Done.

Almost.

She filled a bucket with hot soapy water and went out the back door. The twins were reclining on two white plastic lawn chairs, which they had positioned side by side on the patio. They were faceup; their chins were elevated. Their arms were rigid at their sides. "Do you think it's warm enough out here to get a tan?" Jessica asked without opening her eyes.

"At four-thirty in the afternoon? In December?"

Paige turned her head in Ashley's direction and shaded her eyes with her hand. "Well, this isn't exactly fun, lying out here, you know."

"So why do it, then? There's plenty of other things to do around here, like cleaning the barbecue."

"Ttttuh," Paige answered. "Leave us alone. We already gardened. And we're pooped. As pooped as Pooh bear," she added in a quiet voice. "Aren't we, hunny?" She reached over and nudged Jessica's leg with her foot.

"Do bears really hibernate in holes in the ground?" Jessica asked Ashley. "That's what Paige was trying to tell me."

Ashley ignored her.

"In winter, these magnificent hairy beasts vanish!" Paige announced in a British accent, as if she were narrating a PBS wildlife show.

"Poooohfff!" she said, catching Jessica's eye. "They disappear. Then they reappear— ferociously hungry—in spring!"

"Do they really?" said Jessica. "Extraordinary creatures, aren't they!"

My stepsisters are psychos, decided Ashley. Certifiable, just by looking into their eyes . . .

She surveyed the yard for evidence of their gardening project. In the middle of what one might refer to as the lawn, she noted a small patch of freshly turned dirt, and the sad little Venus flytrap was poking out of the center of it.

Oh, great.

Every single leaf had been lopped off the

daisy plant. The pruning shears lay open on the ground.

"How come you guys cut down the daisy plant? I planted that six months ago, for Phyllis."

"Shhh," said Jessica. "It needed pruning. Paige read it in a nature book. About bears, plants and fish."

"She did not."

Ashley lifted the grill out of the barbecue and brushed it with the wire brush. She cleaned the outside of the barbecue and the lid with soapy water. She dragged the end of the hose over and rinsed it.

Do not spray the twins, she instructed herself. I mean it!

She carefully coiled the hose and flopped it onto the ground next to the faucet.

As she crossed the patio, she noticed that a huge stinkbug was standing on its head with its rear pointing in the direction of the lawn chairs.

"Fire on 'em," Ashley mumbled.

"Huh?" said Paige.

"Nothing."

Jessica lifted her head. "I hear the Nomad!" she cried. "Mommy's home!"

She and Paige turned to each other and made identical, exaggerated happy expressions.

"Our mommy's home!" cried Jessica again. "With our gram-gram!"

The twins jumped to their feet and ran around the side of the house to the front yard. Ashley could hear them squealing like two piglets.

What an act, she thought.

She walked up the back stairs into the house.

Everything was as it should be: The kitchen was toasty; it smelled of baked chicken. The floors were spotless. Ashley leaned down and picked up a piece of lint from the rug before swinging the front door open.

Grammie was already standing on the top step. "Ashley? Oh, my," she said. "Everything Phyllis told me is true—and then some! And yes—you do look like your father! My goodness! Look at those curls!" She gave Ashley a squeeze. "Your hair smells delicious!" she whispered. "Delicious!"

She stepped back and regarded Ashley with a look of pretend suspicion. "You've got Dazzle in it, don't you," she said, peering over the frames of her golden plastic sunglasses.

Ashley shook her head.

"Oh, yes you do," said Grammie, walking into the living room. "You California girls are such cheaters. Those highlights come straight out of a bottle—you can't fool me." She put her arm around Ashley's waist and they strolled across the rug. They were almost exactly the same height. "Five foot one?" Grammie asked.

"Mmmm-hmmmm."

"Size seven shoes?"

"Mmmm-hmmmm."

"Hold up your hand." Grammie matched her hand to Ashley's hand. "We're twins!"

Grammie's nails were polished hot pink, with a splashy abstract design on top, in fluorescent green, gold and black. She wiggled them in the air. "Want me to paint your fingernails?"

"Yes!" said Ashley.

"I was a professional makeup person once—when I worked for *Vogue*. Did Phyllis tell you that?"

Jessica and Paige huffed through the door into the living room, each carrying a suitcase. "We do too!" cried Jessica. Grammie covered her ears and flinched. "We want you to polish *our* nails too. First!" Jessica cried. "I called it!"

"No!" said Paige, elbowing her way past Jessica. "Me!" She jumped in front of Grammie

119

and made a cutie-pie expression, practically in Grammie's face.

Phyllis appeared, carrying a hatbox. "You two nuts," she said with a chuckle. "What'll I do with you?"

How about having them locked up in juvenile hall for a couple of weeks? thought Ashley.

Or maybe sent to a work camp.

"You guys are so competitive," said Phyllis, giving Jessica's ponytail an affectionate tug. She smiled proudly at Grammie. "*Assertive* is what they call it these days."

"Is that so?" said Grammie. She reached up and pinched Paige's nose, clamping it tightly between her thumb and the knuckle of her first finger. "So you think you should be first, huh?"

Paige nodded.

"We'll see about that."

Grammie let go of Paige's nose and gave her cheek a couple of pats—slaps, almost. She turned to Phyllis. "Are you going to stand there with the door wide open?"

"I'll get it!" said Jessica. She quietly shut the door. "Mommy?"

"Yes, kitten?"

"Um—I need to tell you something."

"What."

"Well ..."

"Yes?"

"We *were* going to call you at work and say hi—but Ashley broke the phone," said Jessica, "so we couldn't. But it wasn't really that much her fault—she just lost her patience with us, I think. We were eavesdropping again," she confessed. She made a sad face at Phyllis, and Phyllis made a sad face back.

"But we're not going to do it anymore, we *promise!*" cried Paige. She drew a cross over her heart with her finger.

Phyllis looked at Ashley. "The phone is completely broken?"

"Well—there's no dial tone."

"Again?"

Ashley nodded.

"You had no phone all day? That concerns me! I'm glad I didn't try to call and check in on you guys. It must be that stupid jack in my room—I need to ask Ed Anderson to come back over and take another look at it."

"That old geezer can't fix a phone!" said Jessica. She pretended to laugh into her hand. "Only kidding. Anyway, Paige and I worked in the garden. And guess what?"

"What."

"We have a surprise for you out there!"

And the surprise is a pretty little half-dead meat-eating plant, Ashley added to herself. And also a butchered daisy bush.

"I'm *sure* it can wait until after supper," said Grammie. She offered Ashley her arm and they headed toward the kitchen. "Are you our chef this evening? Mmmmmm-mmmmmm!"

She sniffed the air.

"I could eat a horse!"

Eight

"**E**d was a World War Two paratrooper," Phyllis whispered from behind the *National Enquirer*.

"Oh?" whispered Grammie. She marked her place in the romance novel she was reading and closed the book.

"Yes."

Phyllis folded the corner of the paper down and peered over it at Grammie. "There's a photograph of him in his house," she whispered, "standing next to an airplane. With a whole squadron of paratroopers—Airborne Something-or-another, it says. Wasn't Grandpa in that war?"

Grammie took off her glasses and let them

rest against her blouse on their golden chain. "Phyllis! What a question!" She straightened her collar and lightly touched the top of her silver hairdo. "Yes, he was in 'that war.' So was I!"

Grammie made eye contact with Ashley, who was standing in the kitchen doorway. "Her grandfather flew a P-51 Mustang in World War Two," Grammie whispered across the room.

"I knew that!" whispered Phyllis. "I forgot."

Grammie seemed taken aback. "Forgot?"

"Sor-ry!" whispered Phyllis.

Ashley loudly cleared her throat.

"Excuse me, Ashbucket," said Ed Anderson affectionately. He walked back into the living room. "I think I've solved the problem." He scratched the top of his head—which was hairless, except for a few flyaway gray strands. "The novelty phone was off the hook. In the youngsters' room, behind the bed."

Phyllis looked up at him. "What novelty phone?"

"The leopard-skin high-top Ked back there—or Converse or whatever the heck it is," said Mr. Anderson. "The gosh-darn thing needs to stand straight up on the sole of the shoe to be hung up properly. It was on its side, under the bed. That's how you lost your dial tone."

Phyllis closed the paper and dropped it onto the rug beside the chair. "*That* phone? I thought I tossed that into the Goodwill bag." She looked at Ashley. "It was your dad's. He used to tell us he got 'a kick' out of that phone. Remember?"

"I remember," said Ashley.

Why would Phyllis give Ashley's dad's sneaker phone away without asking Ashley?

"Well, it's hung up now," said Mr. Anderson.

"I'd forgotten there even was a jack in the girls' room," said Phyllis.

"Well, there is. Just above the molding, under the bed." Mr. Anderson put both fists on his waist, looked down at the floor and shook his head. "It's funny, though. Last time I was over, I questioned those duplicate imps of yours as to whether or not there was a phone jack in their room . . . and they said no. Those rascals."

Grammie lifted an eyebrow at Phyllis, and Phyllis looked away.

Mr. Anderson whacked and smacked some dust off the cuffs of his pants, which were well above the high-water mark. "This time, I took a look down there in the crawl space with my

Mag light here." He patted his flashlight, which was hanging from his belt by a hook and looked over at Grammie, who was watching him intently. "Don't leave home without it!" he said with a chuckle.

"Anyway." He began drawing in the air with a couple of crooked fingers. "There's a little box downstairs, right below where the phone line comes into the house—by the fuse box. Three lines come out of it, and I followed 'em with my flashlight and—"

"Thanks, Ed," said Phyllis. She yawned.

There was an awkward silence.

"Well, good night, ladies." Mr. Anderson took his Oakland A's cap out of his back pocket and reshaped it.

"Thank you for coming over," Grammie said politely. She stood up and offered Mr. Anderson her hand. "You're a prince to help us."

Mr. Anderson bowed. "The pleasure is mine." He put on his cap, which bent down the tops of his sizable ears. "Enjoy your stay," he said to Grammie.

"Thank you."

"Will you be here awhile?"

"A couple of days."

"I'm stuck working till four tomorrow," said

Phyllis. "Otherwise I'd take her to lunch—tour her around, show her the sights . . ."

"Well, if you're not available, then let me introduce her to the neighborhood tour guide," said Mr. Anderson. He walked out the door, closing it behind him.

Then he walked back again with his hat on backward. "Anderson Tours," he said. "At your service. Tomorrow's first stop: Fresh Choice. Unless you'd prefer Sizzler."

"No, I enjoy Fresh Choice very much, thank you," said Grammie. "But I'll only go on one condition: You'll let me treat."

"Well, how about Dutch?"

"No. My treat. Or no tour."

"Well, if that's the way you're going to be . . . I won't argue with a lady," said Mr. Anderson. "Eleven-thirty?"

"Eleven-thirty. On the button!" said Grammie.

Mr. Anderson looked at Ashley. "You and the girls want to join us?"

"I don't think so," said Ashley. "But thanks."

She and Grammie exchanged a sly glance.

Grammie lifted her glasses from her bosom to the bridge of her nose, stood on tiptoe and gazed over Mr. Anderson's shoulder. "Now, will you look at that," she said. She moved to the doorway and they both stepped out onto the stoop. A fingernail moon was rising over the rooftops. "I saw that same moon over Miami, just last night."

"Phyllis?" said Ashley quietly.

"Yes?"

"Could I talk to you a minute?"

With a sigh, Phyllis arose from the La-Z-Boy. She put both of her palms on the small of her back, with her thumbs at her waist. She leaned back to stretch. "I'm so tired."

Grammie looked back into the living room. "I bet you are," she called in gently. "You've had a long day. And you know what? I've logged some miles myself. It's midnight, my time. And I'm just about to turn into a pumpkin."

"Phyllis?" said Ashley again.

"What!"

Ashley motioned Phyllis into the kitchen. "You're not going to say *anything* to Jessica and Paige about stealing the phone from the Goodwill bag?" she asked. "And secretly having it in their room?"

Suddenly Paige was in the room. "Shut up," she whispered. "It's none of your business."

"It is, since you've been listening in on my conversations under your bed," Ashley complained.

Phyllis turned to Paige and stared at her with an exasperated expression. "Have you?"

"No. Cross my heart, I haven't."

"Has Jessica?"

Paige shrugged. "I don't know. Ask her when she gets out of the shower. Besides, *Mom*," said Paige, making bug eyes at Phyllis. "If any of us have been listening in on Ashley's conversations, we've been listening in *your* room . . . and you know it."

She began circling Phyllis, eyeing her. "On *your* speaker phone. And you were a co-conspirator," she said. "You even said so yourself."

She opened her lips to smile, and her braces glimmered.

Yikes! thought Ashley. She looks like she's just about to morph into . . . Help! A wild pig! With rabies!

Jessica had walked in and was observing the scene, wearing Phyllis's terry-cloth robe and a towel on her head. She gave Phyllis a look. "Mom-meee?"

"What."

"You know what," said Jessica. She made a *shame, shame* sign with her fingers. "Admit it."

"I was *not* listening," said Phyllis, pursing her lips. "Now, one of you crawl under that bed and fork that sneaker over."

"No! We *need* that phone! And you were only going to give it away!" whined Jessica. "It's ours. We found it in the Goodwill bag, and it's ours."

"Get it. Now."

"But Ashley's always taking the one out of your room," moaned Jessica. "And hogging both phones in the kitchen. Like she did today!"

"Did you?" asked Phyllis in a quiet voice.

"Yes, but—"

"Then drop it," said Phyllis. "Say nighty-night to Grammie. All of you." Phyllis looked sideways at Ashley. "Not *one word* to her about the party," she whispered. "Not tonight, and not tomorrow morning."

"Well, when will you find out if you have child care?" whispered Ashley.

"Tomorrow, by noon. And if you can manage to keep the phones on the hooks, I'll call you and tell you. But for tonight, mum's the word." Phyllis moved her fingers to her lips. "I mean it, Ashley."

The phone rang, and Phyllis reached for it. "Hello? Yes, Ana. But sweetie? It's too late for her to talk—"

"No!" cried Ashley. "Just for one minute!" she pleaded.

Phyllis covered the receiver with her hand. "Say night-night to Grammie," she mouthed.

"I need to—"

"No!" mouthed Phyllis.

"Oh-kay," Phyllis said to Ana. "Yes, okay . . . Fine. Say hi to your mom from me. Tell her happy new year and have fun at the beach. When are you leaving? . . . Ah . . . Ah . . . Ah. Good. So you'll be there early. Yes, I'll tell her. Sure thing."

Phyllis hung up the phone. "It was Ana."

Uh, yes. I gathered that, thought Ashley.

"She says happy new year."

"I wanted to tell her happy new year to her, too," said Ashley. "Can I call her back? Really quick? I need to ask—"

"No, you don't," said Phyllis. "You may *want* to ask her something, but you don't *need* to ask her anything. It's bedtime at their house too—

they're leaving for the coast at eight in the morning. And don't huff at me. Do you want to know what Ana said, or not?"

"Yes, please."

"Well," began Phyllis, "she gave me one of her usual cryptic messages: 'Tell Ashley everything is okay.' Whatever that means. Then— Lilian will be dropping by here sometime tomorrow morning to pick up your share"— Phyllis lowered her voice to a whisper—"of the limo money."

"Lily is coming here?"

"Apparently so."

"What time?"

"Ashley? I'm not your appointments secretary. Please. Get your things so Grammie can get to bed."

Ashley trudged into her room and gathered her nightgown, Froggy, an outfit to wear in the morning, her brush, ponytail tie, hair clips and . . . what else? thought Ashley. My Pooh bank, in case Lily stops by before Grammie wakes up. She opened her closet door.

"Oh, good grief," scoffed Grammie as she walked into the bedroom. "Where did Phyllis dig this up from?" She walked up to the old photograph of herself and peered at it for a long moment. "Taken before gravity hit," she told Ashley, tugging on the wattles under her chin. "Thank you for giving up your room to me," she added. "You're sweet to do it."

Ashley turned around and smiled. "I don't mind," she said quietly.

And Ashley really didn't mind.

"In fact, I'll let Froggy sleep in bed with you." She stroked him briefly, then placed him gently on top of the bedspread, on the pillow.

"He doesn't snore, does he?"

"A little," said Ashley.

"Well, so do I—a little," said Grammie. "So. You're camping on the couch?"

Ashley nodded. "It's comfortable—I don't mind."

"Frightful color, though, don't you think?" whispered Grammie. "Phyllis never did have any color sense. Don't say I said it."

"I won't. Good night."

"No hug?" Ashley gave Grammie a hug. "Sweet dreams," Grammie told her.

Ashley shuffled into the bathroom to change into her nightgown. The plastic bottle of conditioner had tipped over in the tub, and a pink line of goop was heading slowly toward the drain. All the hand towels were rumpled; one had dropped onto the floor. The mirror was steamed, and on it Jessica had drawn a heart with her finger and written *Trevir + Ashley* inside.

Trevor + Ashley.

This combination was seeming less and less possible by the moment. Did he still like her, after the telephone disaster? *Could* he still like her?

Ashley wished more than anything that Phyllis had let her talk to Ana, so she could have found out what Ana had found out when Ana had called Lily.

Maybe Ana had even talked directly to Trevor; maybe Lily had paged him, he'd called her back, and Lily had arranged another conference call—this time to a household inhabited by sane individuals: Ana's.

Or maybe Lily had arranged it so that Trevor called Ana directly.

Or maybe Ana had just plain paged Trevor!

What a rip. Ashley's almost-boyfriend gets paged by her best friend before Ashley even figures out how to page a pager.

But everything is okay, Ashley tried to reassure herself. Ana said—everything's okay.

Ashley looked at the heart on the mirror.

She changed the *i* to an *o*.

And she left it there.

She stepped out of her clothes and slipped into her nightgown.

There was the tiniest rap at the door. "Ashley?"

It sounded like Grammie.

Ashley clutched closed the neck of her flannel nightgown and opened the door a little.

It *was* Grammie! Even shorter now, with no shoes on.

Grammie signaled to her to come out. "They're all in the girls' room; Phyllis is reading a bedtime story. *The House at Pooh Corner.* I asked her to, of course," said Grammie with a wink. "Don't move!" she whispered. She tiptoed past Ashley and turned on the faucet in the bathroom sink; then she pushed in the button on the door handle and closed the door, turning the handle to make sure it was locked. "You're in there brushing your teeth and washing your face," she whispered. "I'll open it with a hairpin later."

Grammie took Ashley's hand and led her down the hall for a few steps, then steered her into Ashley's bedroom.

Grammie quickly unzipped her suitcase and took out four presents, wrapped in paper printed with seashells. "The best one's for you," she whispered. "Open it later. The rest get pajamas."

She slid Ashley's present under the bed.

"Follow me!"

Carrying the other three packages, she led the way out of Ashley's room and down the hall.

Yikes!

What's going on? thought Ashley.

Grammie nodded in the direction of the doorway to Phyllis's room.

"Phyllis thinks because I'm seventy-something I can't hear," she whispered as they tiptoed in. "But I'm as sharp as a tack—and I always have been. Especially when it comes to Phyllis and her controlling behavior patterns. But don't worry—I've got you covered. And I'm pulling rank!"

Grammie pointed to the phone. A rhinestone glued to her fingernail winked.

"Call your friend," she commanded in a whisper. "There's no reason on earth why you can't wish a friend a happy new year."

Ashley's eyes grew round.

"Just do it!" whispered Grammie. She snuck out and closed the door.

"Phyllis?" Ashley heard Grammie call out in a loud voice. "And Paige and Jessica? Stay where you are—special delivery! I come bearing gifts from the land of sunshine!"

Ashley heard squeals and several loud thumps.

"And we're opening them one at a time!" she heard Grammie say sternly. "Phyllis? Yours will be first. Girls? Back off!"

The house grew quiet.

Ashley could hear the distant sound of water running into the bathroom sink. And Grammie, launching into what was apparently going to be a lengthy introduction to Phyllis's gift.

Ashley stared at the phone.

Her heart was racing.

All you have to do is pick up that receiver, she told herself. And press seven numbers . . . that's all you have to do.

She heard paper tearing, then a few ooohs and ahhhhs.

Hurry up!

She walked closer to Phyllis's nightstand. She put her hand on the receiver.

She glanced over her shoulder at the door.

Would she dare?

Nine

Ashley opened her eyes.

The world had turned orange.

Where am I?

Who am I?

She sat up. Grammie was sitting in the La-Z-Boy in her white robe and slippers, holding a cup of tea. The curtains were open behind her, and light was flooding in. The sky was bright blue. Grammie's hair was lit like a silver cloud.

"I was enjoying sitting here, watching you sleep," she quietly told Ashley. She took a sip of tea. "Like Sleeping Beauty!"

She checked her watch.

"I thought I might have to find a prince to wake you up."

Ashley yawned. "Is it okay if I get my Pooh bank out of my closet?"

"Of course."

"What time is it?"

"Ten-thirty."

"Already?"

Ashley sat on the edge of the couch for a moment to wake up before padding barefoot into her room. She could hear squawks and cheers coming from the TV set in the girls' room. A morning talk show—strictly prohibited by Phyllis, not that Paige or Jessica cared.

Ashley eyed Froggy, elegantly posed on the pillow with his front feet crossed one over the other.

See? she told herself. You're not neurotic. You had only the smallest amount of separation anxiety during your night away from Froggy.

You were thirty feet away from him, on a couch! she told herself.

She opened her closet door and yawned two more times. She parted some hangers and looked at her little black dress in its thin plastic bag from the dry cleaners.

She needed to locate and polish her shoes

139

later. But before she had a shower—so she wouldn't get shoe polish under her nails.

She looked down at the cardboard box that held her treasures. Her diary was right on top, waiting to be invaded by Paige and Jessica. It didn't matter; Ashley would never write another word in it for the rest of her life.

Actually . . .

Maybe she would!

She took the key from around her neck, unlocked her diary and flipped it open.

She rummaged through her treasures and found a pen.

She searched for the first empty page and nibbled on the top of the pen before writing in her most beautiful, flowery cursive:

Dear loo-sahs,
This is just a happy little note to say, hey—
I hope you enjoy staying home tonight while I
go to the biggest, best party ever.

A smile crept across Ashley's face.

If you're reading this before midnight, let
me take the time to say—Boring New Year!
to both of you. If you're reading this after

New Year's, I'd just like to say that I hope your New Year's Eve was totally uneventful, and may you have many more boring New Year's Eves to come. A whole millennium full!

If that was how you spelled *millennium*—not that the twins would know.

She signed it:

Ha! Ha! Ashley E. Toral
P.S. Ever wondered why I never unlock your diaries and read them? Too boring! Got a life.

Ashley signed happily and shut and locked the diary.

Good for you, she told herself. It's time you stood up.

I'm proud of you!

Oh yes. We like the new me, Ashley told herself. Very, very much. Breaking the rules last night by phoning Ana was *just* what the doctor ordered.

She closed her eyes.

And hearing what Ana said about Trevor was also just what the doctor ordered.

Ashley had fallen asleep with it in her heart:

"Tell her I'll call her from the limo—I think it will be about seven-thirty. And ask her . . ." He had stopped talking at this point, according to Ana.

"Nothing. I'll ask her myself," he had said.

And Ana suspected that he wanted to ask Ashley to go out.

Would he?

Get money. Get dressed, Ashley told herself. Lily will be here in thirty minutes. You've got to casually hang a dishtowel over the mailbox to hide the street number and be casually milling around in front of Mr. Anderson's house in thirty minutes.

Not too close to the gnomes.

Go! she told herself.

But wait a minute . . .

Her treasure box looked . . . emptier than it should.

Where was her Pooh bank?

She rummaged through the box.

But of course it wasn't in the box! Where would it be, under the pencils? Inside a two-inch-by-two-inch-by-two-inch ceramic Piglet jar?

It wasn't in the box!

Ashley rummaged through the shoes behind

the box, and the stuff beside the shoes. Back, back, back into the depths of the closet she rummaged, breathing more and more heavily.

She tipped backward and sat on the rug. Then she brought her knees up inside her nightgown and hugged them and rested her cheek on one knee.

"Everything okay?" said a small voice in the doorway.

"Yes," lied Ashley.

"I think I'll take a quick shower, then—to get ready for my . . . *date!*"

Ashley forced a smile.

Grammie pretended to swoon, for Ashley's benefit. "I've always loved a military man," she whispered. "I wish Ed would wear his flight jacket! And a white silk scarf!"

She gathered a few things and went into the bathroom, humming.

Ashley waited until she heard the shower running. Then she stood up, stormed the twins' room, turned off the TV and looked at them. "Where's. My. *Pooh bank!*"

"Shut up. We don't know anything about any Pooh bank," said Paige. "Keep track of your own stuff." She picked up the remote and clicked the TV back on. Two women in tight dresses were rolling around on the floor pulling each other's hair.

Ashley yanked open Paige's chest of drawers and began throwing the contents over her shoulder and onto the floor.

"Stop!"

"Shhh!" said Jessica, who was close to Paige on Paige's bed. "Look! The security guards are trying to pull them apart!"

Ashley then searched Jessica's dresser, methodically emptying it, drawer by drawer.

By drawer.

"I hope you know," said Jessica, without taking her eyes off the screen, "that you're picking all that stuff up."

Ashley dumped out the hamper and spread the dirty clothes around.

She glanced up at the TV. " 'Nightmare Sisters' " a silver-haired man was saying into the microphone he was holding, "will be back, after this brief message."

"Hey! It's a show about you guys!" Ashley sang out cheerily. "Keep watching—at the rate you're going, you'll be ready to make an appearance in five or ten years!"

Nobody heard this but Ashley. Or at least, so the twins pretended. Paige had picked up the remote and turned up the volume to drown Ashley out.

Ashley ransacked the closet, chucking shoes, boots, belts and toys onto the rug behind her, while the twins sang along to a commercial at the tops of their lungs.

Ashley pulled the blankets off Jessica's bed and shook them out. She peered underneath the bed.

Then she picked up the dust ruffle, plunged under Paige's bed headfirst and wriggled toward the wall. "And this. Was. My. Father's. Phone. So. It's. Mine! Not yours!" she shouted, not that they heard her.

She reached to unclip the shoe phone line from the jack—but at that exact moment, it rang.

Very softly.

"Hello?" said Ashley, under the bed. She smelled the old rubber sole of the tennis shoe. Where was her ear supposed to go? She turned the phone around and rolled onto her back. "Hello?"

She looked up at the threads that hung down from the box springs like spiderwebs.

"Kitten?"

It was Phyllis.

"Is that you?"

"It's Ashley."

"Oh. What's the matter?"

"The twins stole my limo money, that's what."

"I can barely hear you," said Phyllis. "What's the commotion? Is that the twins? Where *are* you, Ashley? You sound like you're talking from inside a barrel!"

"The twins stole my limo money!" shouted Ashley.

The TV instantly went silent.

"Well," said Phyllis. "They'll give it back. I'll talk to them in just one minute and they'll give it back, I promise you. Ashley? I have to tell you: You were right, right, right! about Sarah Cranston. She stopped by the office and I just caught her hurrying out the door."

Ohboy, thought Ashley.

"She was in a terrible rush, but I snagged her to have coffee. And she said yes. Isn't that sweet?"

"I guess . . ."

"What do you mean, you guess?" said Phyllis. "This woman takes twenty minutes out of a very, very busy day to chat with me. We had coffee—just the two of us, down by the espresso cart near the main entrance. You know that little cart?"

"Um hmmm."

"Well, we each had a latte—she paid for both. Groovy, huh?"

Ashley didn't respond.

"And I told her about our family dilemma," continued Phyllis. "I just spilled my guts to her—about Grammie, and the flight phobia, and the crash that caused it, that took my mom and dad, so many years ago—"

Great. Just great, thought Ashley. Tell Grammie's business to everybody, tell your business to everybody . . .

"—and how I couldn't get off work today," said Phyllis, "and the child care problem for tonight, and guess what?"

Ashley froze.

"What."

"*What* a class act this woman is," said Phyllis.

Please, no, thought Ashley.

"Whaddya think she said?" said Phyllis. "Just tell me: Whaddya think? Just make one guess."

Please, please . . . no, thought Ashley. Say it isn't true.

"She said the girls are welcome to come to the party!"

Ashley's heart started beating double-time.

"Isn't that great?" gushed Phyllis. "I'm so relieved—for all of us. They can wear their black dresses—I know, I know, they're similar to yours, but you can accessorize differently."

Breathe! Ashley told herself.

Talk!

Say something!

She heard muffled squeaks and squeals. The twins were listening in!

"Look," said Phyllis. "Let me not be insensitive here. I *completely* understand if you don't want them to go with you in the limo—as a matter of fact, even if you said yes I'd say no."

You're dreaming this—this is a nightmare.

Wake up!

Right now!

"And you'll be proud of me, Ashles. I did *not* offer to be half-time chauffeur—except that I told her I *would* drop the twins off at Ocean Crest, a little early—which she said was fine."

Speak!

"Ashley? Are you listening? Grammie and I," continued Phyllis, now bubbling over with excitement, "will swing by and pick them up again just before midnight. Grammie's so cranky, and she could use the beauty rest, so why keep her up till midnight? Are you there? Regardless, I don't want my two babies out on the town—that Y2K computer shutdown stuff scares me to death. Honey?"

Breathe! Ashley told herself again.

"But don't you worry that pretty little head of yours. *You* can stay past midnight and come home in the limo with your pals. Whenever. The aunt's supervising—the aunt's driving— what do I care?" said Phyllis, now quite giddy. "You're the eldest of *my* three children, and you're entitled to the privileges that go along with that territory. Ashley? Are you there?"

"She's there," said a voice on the phone. "She's listening in, under my bed, on the shoe phone. And Mommy?"

"Yes, sweetheart?"

"Thank you sooooo much," said Paige.

"Well, you two be good, though," said Phyllis, pretending to be stern. "This party is really for the older kids. Even Ana and Emily didn't get invited, so behave! And *immediately* give Ashley back her limo money."

"Okay, Mommy," said Paige. "We were only joking. We were just about to give it back, even if you didn't ask us to. But Mommy?"

"What."

"Ashley isn't *really* one of your *real* children, is she?"

"Ashley? Are you listening?" said Phyllis. "Get out from under that bed and get on a regular phone so you can participate in this conversation."

"But Mommy?" said Jessica. "Can we please, please, please go in the limo?"

"No. Absolutely not. I want to pick you up myself. Is this Jessica now? Get off the phone." Phyllis paused. "It's not on speaker, is it? It better not be!" She lowered her voice. "Where's Grammie?"

Ashley put the shoe down carefully in the upright position so she would be sure it hung up. She lay on her back on the rug, looking up. Tears were running down the sides of her face and around the backs of her ears. Her whole body was trembling.

Jessica peered under the bed at Ashley. "Pooh's outside—hibernating under the Venus flytrap." She clicked on a flashlight and shined it into Ashley's face. "And don't be such a crybaby.

150

He's plastic—completely washable and you know it. It was just a joke, Ashley. Lighten up."

Paige's face appeared, upside down. "And get out of our room," she added. "We'll clean up the mess you made—ourselves. You pig." She pulled up the tip of her nose with her finger and started grunting.

Ashley crept out from under the bed and went out the back door. Jessica rapped on the window and waved as Ashley dug up and brushed off Pooh.

Ashley took a moment to replant the flytrap in a shady spot, near the edge of the patio. Because there *was,* as it turned out, a bright green shoot with a hairy, flat trap on the end of it. And it was open. So full of hope!

Maybe it would survive.

Ashley rinsed off Pooh under the kitchen faucet, careful not to get water in the coin slot.

She carried him into the living room.

"Grammie?"

"Yes?"

"You look nice."

"Why, thank you, Ashley."

Ashley sat down at the table next to the window, where Grammie was seated, wearing a round magnifying mirror hooked around her neck. She was holding a small black mascara wand close to her eyelashes. She slowly blinked as she turned the bristles and moved the wand upward. "I learned this when I worked for *Vogue*," she whispered without looking at Ashley. "I'm careful about makeup."

She slowly blinked again.

And again.

"I don't want to look like one of those ancient ladies who generalize with makeup: dark lines in the general area of eyes and eyelids, dark arches above 'em—never mind where the actual eyebrows are growing."

She chuckled.

"Pink or plum-colored circles in the vicinity of the cheeks. Red on and around the lips."

She looked sideways at Ashley.

"Look at me! Getting all gussied up to go to Fresh Choice." She dipped the mascara wand into the holder. "With a handsome prince and former paratrooper. But he *does* have some intense blue peepers, doesn't he."

"Yup," said Ashley.

"And I like the cookie duster. Do you?"

"The mustache? Yup."

"You think he'll get fresh in Fresh Choice? I hope so!" Grammie said before Ashley could

152

answer. "I'm not just going for the garbanzo beans and ranch dressing."

Ashley put her Pooh bank in front of her. She dried him off with a dishtowel. Then she turned him upside down and pulled the rubber plug out of the hole on the bottom. She shook out her lucky fifty-cent piece and pulled out the ten two-dollar bills. "Could you do me a favor?"

Hang on now, she told herself.

"Of course I could!"

Grammie uncapped her lipstick and rolled it partway up. She looked into the mirror again and slowly drew a perfect red lip line, slightly extending her upper lip to make a bow shape.

She pressed her lips together and looked again at Ashley.

"Will you please give this money"—Ashley stood up and took $14.50 out of her pocket, and added it to the $20.50 she had in her hand—"to a girl named Lily, who's probably going to come honk outside the door in about five minutes."

Don't lose it, Ashley told herself. Just stay in control. You've made your decision, so stick to it.

"And please tell her that I can't go," she said

cheerily, "but I'm paying anyway. Because I promised I would. Somebody's dad is depending on the money. That's all I want you to say."

Ashley put the wad of money on the table and pushed it closer to Grammie's makeup bag. "And I don't want you to ask me anything else."

Grammie kept looking straight at Ashley.

And Ashley kept looking straight at Grammie.

And Ashley's mouth began to wobble, and her breathing grew unsteady. And soon the room got blurry. She blinked to clear the picture.

"Why can't you go?" asked Grammie.

"I can't!" said Ashley. "I just can't, that's all—and I can't talk about it."

"Yes, you can," said Grammie. "You can go, and I can stay here with the twins. Phyllis and I will have a glass of champagne with Ed in the garden and call it a night."

"You're not supposed to know about any of this!" said Ashley.

"Then Phyllis should teach her daughters not to put the phone on speaker and yap into it while her cranky grandmother is within earshot. After having gotten lots of beauty rest—which Phyllis apparently feels I need more of, at age seventy-five."

"You can't stay here—you can't spoil Phyllis's New Year's Eve!"

"Yes, I can."

"I don't want you to," said Ashley. "It's not worth it."

"Yes, it is."

"No—it really isn't. Please, *somebody* just for once listen to me. I'm not going to the party. My shoes won't fit. My dress is so awful, even my sisters like it—so much they bought dresses almost exactly the same!"

Grammie shook her head.

"Phyllis is so stressed—she works so hard," said Ashley. "She's barely hanging on! Haven't you noticed?"

"As a matter of fact . . . ," said Grammie. She nodded.

"And she so much wants you two to have a good New Year's Eve together!" cried Ashley. "At the Shangri-La Room."

Grammie made a terrible face.

"Promise me," said Ashley, "you won't let her know you know about the party. I'm staying home—I'll miss the party." She paused. "But for once—*just for once,*" she said with true longing in her voice. "I'm going to spoil something for the twins. They won't get to go to the party either."

A faraway look came into Ashley's eyes. "The dance is already ruined for me, anyway. I should have gone with Ana and Emily to the beach. That's where I belong, with my real friends—my friends who care about me."

"I understand how you feel," said Grammie. She reached over, put her hand on Ashley's arm and patted it. "Is it too late to go along with them?" she quietly asked.

"Yeah," sighed Ashley. "They left. Hours ago."

"Do you know where they're staying? Where is it? Maybe Ed and I could take a ride over there and drop you off."

"Well, it's only about half an hour from here," said Ashley. "And I could probably find the cabin—they rented it once before, and I stayed with them. But there's one minor detail. Actually, two minor details."

"Oh," said Grammie. "Right."

Ashley looked down at Grammie's beautiful painted nails resting on her arm.

"Go to the party, Ashley. Ignore the twins!

Let me paint your nails for you; I can do it in a flash. You like pastels? I'll go out to lunch with Ed and pick up some polish and be back in time. When's the limo coming?"

There was a beep outside the door.

"It isn't," said Ashley. "The limo isn't going to be coming. Quick! It's Lily!" Ashley picked up the money, put it into Grammie's hand and gently wrapped her fingers around it.

"You're sure about this?" said Grammie.

Ashley hesitated.

"Yes."

"Okay, then." Grammie stood up and straightened her skirt. She clipped on her earrings as she walked toward the door. "You're positive?"

Ashley nodded.

Grammie put her hand on the doorknob. "Absolutely?"

"No! Wait!" cried Ashley. "Don't forget to take off the mirror."

She helped Grammie lift off the makeup mirror. She gently put a few of Grammie's silver hairs back in place. "I'm positive. It's better this way." She opened the door for Grammie. "Don't look back!" she whispered. "I don't want Lily to know I'm here!"

"I won't," said Grammie. "I never do. But—will you?"

"Will I what?" said Ashley.

"Will you look back, with regrets, on this last day of the twentieth century?"

"No," said Ashley. "I won't have regrets."

"Well then, how about—on the very first day of the twenty-first century? Will you look back on that day with regrets?"

"I don't know how I'll feel on that day," said Ashley. "I barely know how I feel today."

She paused.

"But . . . maybe I *will* take back that fifty-cent piece. It *is* kind of lucky."

Grammie pressed the fifty-cent piece into Ashley's palm.

The horn beeped again.

And Grammie walked out the door.

Ten

Ashley heard Phyllis come into the house and gasp. "Oh, goodness!" she cried out. "Aren't *we* lovely!"

Ashley opened her bedroom door a crack to listen.

Jessica spoke in a low voice. "Look at my lashes, Mommy! I borrowed Grammie's mascara. Think she'll mind?"

"Well, if she didn't want to share, she shouldn't have left her makeup kit on the table!" whispered Paige.

"You sillies," whispered Phyllis.

Ashley strolled out in her sweats and a raggedy old T-shirt that had once belonged to her dad. "Hi," she said in a casual way. "How was work?"

Phyllis frowned. "You haven't started getting ready? It's six-ten. Where's Grammie? We're supposed to be at the Shangri-La Room by eight or the place will fill up!"

"She called and said to tell you she'd be home pretty soon. She's with Ed Anderson."

"Well, I gathered *that*!" said Phyllis, with a grand roll of her eyeballs. "Why haven't you started to get ready?"

"Me?" said Ashley. "I'm not going."

"What do you mean—you're not going?"

What else could I mean? thought Ashley.

"Just that," she told Phyllis. "What I mean is: I'm not going. I'm fine to stay home and watch the twins. I'm not down for the party anymore."

Paige and Jessica turned and dropped their mouths open, very wide. "Uh!" they said in unison. Each of them put one hand on her hip. "Is she serious?" they said to each other with one voice. Each of them brought the other hand up and rested her fingertips on her cheek, mirroring each other's movements—like the wicked queen in *Snow White*.

They turned to Phyllis. "But Mom!" said Paige. "We're, like, totally *pumped* to go!"

"We're already *dressed*," said Jessica.

And yes, the twins were most certainly already dressed—in their matching black dresses that matched Ashley's black dress, not sort of, but exactly—and pantyhose. And black dolly shoes, and Ashley's pink lipstick. And lost body glitter.

"Go change," Ashley calmly told them.

Phyllis walked a couple of steps closer to Ashley. "What do you mean you're not 'down for' the party anymore?"

"I decided you're right," said Ashley. "I decided I don't like the snob factor either."

"What snob factor! What are you talking about!"

"I don't want to go to a party that excludes my two best friends," said Ashley quietly.

And includes my stepsisters, she added to herself. Wearing dresses identical to mine.

Phyllis dogged Ashley for a long, long moment. "Do you realize what you put me through?" she said. "To arrange it so you could go to this event?"

"Sorry," said Ashley. "But—oh well!" she

said, eyeing the twins. "I don't want to go to a party that excludes people," she went on. "I don't want to go to a party for royalty, in a snootish country club—for kids in with the in crowd. And I don't want to be in with the in crowd. I want to stay home, with my sisters."

Who are totally out of it, she added to herself.

She gazed at Phyllis and Phyllis gazed at her, and neither looked away.

"You're manipulating me," said Phyllis. "You think I just fell off a turnip truck? You're not going because you don't want the girls to go— you want to spoil the evening for them. And for me!"

"That's not true!" lied Ashley.

"You think I'll enjoy myself going out with Grammie, knowing my two girls are sitting at home with a grumpy teen?" said Phyllis, now getting quite wild-eyed.

"What do you mean?" said Ashley. "We'll have fun! The girls and me—we're gonna kick it. Aren't we?"

Paige and Jessica stared at Ashley.

"Honestly!" said Ashley. "I don't feel grumpy—do I look grumpy? We'll watch movies. And eat frozen pizzas—they're only mildly freezer burned. I checked them out when I was cleaning out the fridge—"

She looked sideways at Jessica.

"While the twins were tanning, yesterday. At four-thirty in the afternoon. Or was it when I was scrubbing the barbecue?"

She smiled a small, fake smile at Paige.

"And admiring the dead Venus flytrap they planted on top of the Pooh bank they buried in the dirt. That my mom gave me when I was three."

I can't believe you just said that! thought Ashley.

"Come *on*! We'll eat pizza!" she chirped. "And chill with some chilled prune juice. We three will hang out. Right, guys? It'll be a blast, Phyllis!"

A real hoot, in fact, thought Ashley.

"Go on, girls," she told Paige and Jessica. "Scoot! Change into something more comfortable. Like your jam-jams that your gram-gram gave you."

Phyllis marched over to the table and picked up her keys.

"Girls? Get in the car." She pointed at the door with one skinny finger. "Wait!" She rummaged through a shopping bag. "I picked these up for you on my way home from work." She pulled out two dorky black velvet jackets trimmed with faux fur. "Put them on. Wait!"

Phyllis bit through the plastic label holders with her pointy eyeteeth—fangs, actually. She tossed the labels onto the table.

"You won't be needing yours," she said without looking at Ashley. "They were 'buy two, get one free,' but so what. You're not going to the party so I'll *just* return it."

The twins grabbed their jackets. "Thank you, Mommy!" said Jessica. "Mmmmmm! Paige, feel. They're sooooo soft."

Jessica and Paige rubbed their cheeks against the fur before putting the jackets on.

"And there are these," said Phyllis, pulling out a wad of three horrid black velvet evening shoulder bags, with handles and tags all tangled up.

"What a mess," she mumbled. She unsnarled two of them and threw the third one back into the bag.

"Where's the lipstick?" Ashley heard Jessica whisper as Paige shoved her out the door.

"Wait!" whispered Paige. "I forgot something." She scurried back in the direction of her room. Ashley heard the clattering of her shoes as she scrambled down the hall.

It was quiet for a moment.

Then Paige darted across the living room rug and hurried out the front door again.

Phyllis rolled closed the top of the shopping bag and tossed it onto a chair. "Were you planning to make me look bad in front of my grammie?" she asked Ashley. "Well, it didn't work." She picked up her purse.

"Did it?" she asked, reaching for the doorknob. "Or—were you planning to make me look bad in front of my new friend, Sarah Cranston? That woman is a saint. A saint! When you RSVP a party, kiddo, you don't cancel out at the last minute. You're a no-show—but not everybody in this family is. You're a no-show by your own choice."

Ashley said nothing.

"But just remember tonight," said Phyllis, arching an eyebrow at Ashley.

As if Ashley would ever be able to forget it.

"Tonight, you're making a decision," said Phyllis. "And life is all about decisions. You're making a decision to stay home from a party, you're saying no to watching the sun rise on the year 2000."

Ashley was numb.

She could have watched the sun rise with the other kids?

The twins blasted the horn.

"All because you lack *esprit de corps,*" continued Phyllis. "You deny the twins the opportunity to be real sisters to you; you deny me the opportunity to be a supportive and interested parent. That jacket over there?"—Phyllis nodded in the direction of the shopping bag—"is a symbol of everything that's wrong between us. I bought it so you'd be warm tonight." Phyllis's voice became unsteady. "So I could think of the three of you as my triplets, toasty and warm— and together."

Uh-oh! Chin again! thought Ashley.

"Really together," blubbered Phyllis, "on the eve of the new millennium. You *like* being on the outside—you *want* to be different from us!"

She took a deep breath and gathered herself. Then she whipped her head around and closed the door in Ashley's face. "Yes, darlings!" Ashley heard her sing out from the stoop. "Mommy's coming!"

Ashley just stood there, staring at the rug. She heard the car start; she heard the Nomad's muffler grow fainter and fainter.

The house grew quiet.

She wandered into her bedroom and sat on the edge of her bed. She looked around for Froggy.

He was gone.

On her pillow, opened, was her diary. It was turned to the page she'd written for the twins.

Ashley flopped backward onto her bedspread.

No tears fell. She was way past tears. She stared up at the ceiling.

Where was Trevor?

She didn't know. And she would never know—not tonight, not ever. She tried to picture him in a tux—it was easy, actually. In a tux, with a black bow tie. To match his cummerbund.

She had to close her eyes to see his eyes and dark eyelashes.

She saw his mouth.

"Ashley?"

Grammie was standing in the doorway. "Look what I found at the mall! The cutest thing!"

Ashley sat up. She saw Ed Anderson, standing behind Grammie with his hand on her shoulder.

"Oh, hi," said Ashley.

He smiled and wandered into the living room.

"Where are Phyllis and the girls?" asked Grammie.

"She took them to the party without me."

"How predictable," Grammie groaned. "And she'll pick them up just before midnight, right?"

"I guess so. She's afraid of the Y2K computer crash," said Ashley. She looked down at her hands. "She said it was okay for me to be out later, though. I guess she doesn't care that much about me. When it comes right down to it."

"Ashley? Yes, she does. She is *not* afraid of a computer crash. She's nosy, that's all. It's an excuse for her to come to the party—she'll stroll in, looking for the girls, and—gee, *what a co-inky-dink!* She'll be right there in the middle of everything, just when the clock strikes twelve."

Grammie crossed the rug. "She *does* care about you. She knows you'll be perfectly safe at the party. And perfectly safe in the limo. She even told me somebody's aunt is driving. Right?"

"Right."

"Well, I know Phyllis. Her Y2K fear is nothing more than a convenient excuse for her to show up at the party. But let's not get into Phyllis right now. I've got a little story to tell you."

"After Fresh Choice," began Grammie, "as if we hadn't had enough to eat, Ed and I decided to go to the Starr's cafe for an iced coffee. On our way in, I saw something . . . a mannequin, just your size. And I met a lovely silver-haired woman, and she spoke to me. We could have been sisters, this woman and I!"

Grammie handed Ashley a Starr's shopping bag with paper handles.

Ashley peered into the folds of the crumpled tissue paper inside.

"She joked that I could be a fairy godmother—for two thousand. If I had a fairy godchild. Imagine—little old me, a fairy godmother."

Ashley saw something glimmer.

"A fairy godmother—for two thousand? I thought," said Grammie. "I decided it would be cheap at twice the price. So I took her up on it."

Ashley reached into the bag. She rustled through the paper.

"I'm crossing my fingers that it will fit," said Grammie.

Ashley lifted out the twinkly dress. "You bought me this dress?" she whispered.

And the beaded evening bag.

"And this little purse?"

"Keep digging," said Grammie.

A shoe box was at the bottom of the bag. Ashley lifted the lid. She saw one Italian high-heel shoe; the other was nestled beside it. "You did *not* buy all these things for me!" she whispered.

Grammie clicked open her large straw purse. "I didn't stop there," she said. She passed Ashley a small bag. In it was a little silver box that had MILLENNIUM—BY GUESS? scrawled artfully on the side.

"Thank you," said Ashley. "So much!" She smelled the box. "But Grammie?"

"Yes?"

"You didn't need to buy me all these things. I didn't really stay home because of my dress. I really do like my little black dress—that wasn't the problem! It's just that—"

Grammie raised her hand in the Stop! position. "Here's a little secret, just between the two of us," she whispered. She moved her hand over her heart and patted her chest. "You ready?"

Ashley stared at her.

"I won the lottery three weeks ago in Florida!"

Ashley's eyes grew wider. "You *did*?"

"Yes! On a five-dollar quick-pick."

"You won *the lottery*?"

Grammie shook her head as if she still couldn't believe it. "*I'm* the one with a fairy godmother out there somewhere," she softly told Ashley. "And I must say, she's a mighty generous one, at that! But I haven't told Phyllis yet. I need to think about how to best help Phyllis."

"*You actually won the lottery?*"

"And don't tell Ed!" whispered Grammie. "I want him to fall in love with me—before he knows I'm a wealthy woman—and beg me to move out to California! Isn't he a prince?"

"You'd move out here? To be close to Ed?"

"Well, more to be close to you," said Grammie. "And Phyllis and the girls. Phyllis needs all the help she can get. She needs counseling and parenting skills. And money-managing skills!

"And she needs me," Grammie added quietly. "And I need her. And so do you. And so do the twins. We need each other. There's a house for rent across the street. I've already called about it."

Grammie reached back into her purse. She carefully took out a small paper Starr's bag. Inside was a pale blue jewelry box. She clicked back the lid.

"Dragonflies!" said Grammie. "Necklace, earrings and hair clips—to pin up that beautiful mop of curls! The same lovely woman offered to be my accessories consultant. Celeste something . . .

"And let me tell you! She could sell the Golden Gate Bridge! She reminded me that tonight can only happen once in a thousand years. Plus, she gave me a discount. Like 'em?"

"Do I *like* them?"

Grammie checked her watch. "It's six-forty-five." She locked eyes with Ashley. "What are you waiting for?"

Ashley's shoulders slumped. "It's too late. I told them I wasn't going!"

"You've just changed your mind," said Grammie. "There's a phone in the limo, isn't there?"

Ashley looked down at the dragonflies. They winked and blinked at her.

"And your boy has a pager—doesn't he? Phyllis said he has a pager."

Gosh.

What a blabbermouth Phyllis was!

Grammie reached into her purse again. "This is yours too."

She shook a tiny, flat cell phone out of a silky black bag and flipped it open for Ashley. A green light went on. "See? You've got your own phone. And your own number: It's 143-2000. Calls are free after five and free on the weekends. The monthly bill will be sent to me."

Grammie seemed very pleased with herself. She drummed her fingers on her knee. "You can even play video games on it."

"You got me a *cell phone*?" said Ashley.

Grammie closed her eyes and smiled and nodded.

"It's digital. And you can snap off and snap on any one of the 'five bold colors' that come with it! Everything's in the box in the other room."

"Grammie. You shouldn't have bought me all of these things! I can't let you spend so much money on me," said Ashley. "I mean it. Even if you *did* win the lottery."

"*You* can't let *me*? Who's in charge here? You or me?"

"You," said Ashley.

"Page him," said Grammie.

Ashley stared at the phone in her hand. "I don't know how."

"Let's see . . . Press On," said Grammie. She pressed On for Ashley. "What's his pager number. Do you know it? Of course you know it!"

Ashley pressed 5-5-5-0-0-8-8.

"Now . . . press Send," said Grammie. She poked the Send button with one long, lovely nail. And threw back Ashley's beautiful curls, and held the phone against Ashley's ear. "The number will ring . . . Is it ringing?"

"I heard a beep!" said Ashley.

"Then . . . Type in your number. Quick!" said Grammie.

Ashley held the phone in front of her and pushed 1-4-3-2-0-0-0. "Now press the pound sign," said Grammie.

Ashley pressed it. "And hang up," said Grammie. She reached over and helped Ashley close the phone. "See? We did it! I practiced it several times in the phone store." She folded her hands in her lap and looked at Ashley from over the top of her glasses. "The 1-4-3—that stands for 'I love you.' In pager code."

I'm not following this, but so what, thought Ashley.

"Right?" said Grammie. "Of course I'm right! I read all about pager code in a *Teen Magazine* somebody left in the seat pocket of the airplane." Grammie put her arm around Ashley's shoulder and gave her a squeeze. "Am I way cool?"

Ashley gave Grammie a big, fat kiss on the cheek. "You *so* are!"

"I'm *so* not wanting your boy's pager to be turned off," said Grammie. "It *so* better be on." She looked sideways at Ashley. "Am I good at *Teen Magazine* talk?"

Well . . .

"Yup," lied Ashley.

Her heart was racing. Could Trevor have turned off his pager?

She and Grammie sat close together without speaking.

Grammie checked her watch. A minute passed, and then another one.

Pleasepleasepleasepleaseplease, thought Ashley.

The phone rang.

Grammie tiptoed out and closed the door behind her.

Eleven

"Is your lucky coin in your purse?" asked Grammie.

"Mmmmm-hmmm."

"Is your phone? Stay still!"

"Mmmm-hmmm."

"How about your perfume?"

"Mmmmm."

"Lipstick?"

"Mmmmm."

The phone rang in the kitchen.

"Hold this," Grammie told Ashley, handing her the mascara applicator. "And don't move. Those rhinestones need another minute or two for the glue to harden."

Ashley sat very still. And held the golden

cap of the mascara wand very gently. She peered at her fingernails: On each was painted Grammie's rendition of a sunrise, with a rhinestone Venus twinkling at the tip.

Were they awful or great?

Ashley wasn't sure.

She eyeballed the makeup kit Grammie had brought her from Florida—the present wrapped in seashell paper that she'd forgotten to open until half an hour ago: eye shadow, eyebrow pencil, eyeliner, lip liner, lipstick, blush, oil-free powder, oil-free concealer.

The kit included four small promotional samples of the Fairy Dust Glitter Gel collection— silver, gold, pink and lavender. Good thing, because the twins had absconded with Ashley's body glitter, completely. It was probably in the same place as Froggy. Wherever he was— poor guy.

Grammie had walked into the kitchen and picked up the wall phone.

"Hello?" Ashley heard her say in the background. "No—this is her grandmother, actually. Ah." Grammie frowned as she listened. "Barbecued chicken wings? Oh." She paused to listen. "Uh-oh. No. Well, I'm glad the other guests hadn't arrived yet." She frowned more deeply.

What is going on? wondered Ashley.

"Hmmm. Barbecue sauce?" said Grammie. "And on the deejay, too? That's a shame. Yes, I'll tell her—the minute she walks in the door. Ah. I'm *so* sorry! Did they break anything?"

Grammie caught Ashley's eye. She made a frightful face and pointed to the receiver. "No. Yes! Phyllis will *completely* understand—I can assure you." Grammie put her hand on her forehead. "How awful! I wonder what came over those two! Too much excitement, maybe. Yes. Goodbye."

Grammie hung up the phone. "That was a Mrs. Cranston," she called to Ashley as she walked back into the living room.

What happened?

"She requested," began Grammie, taking the mascara wand from Ashley, "that I be so kind as to tell Phyllis to come right back up to the Ocean Crest Country Club and pick up the twins."

Ashley stared at her.

"It seems they got into a bit of a food fight in the kitchen—and then one dunked the other.

According to Mrs. Cranston, who sounded *quite* cross, they were 'helping out' the caterer, since they were there so early.

"Bring two uninvited guests to a party—almost an hour early? What's wrong with Phyllis!" Grammie wondered out loud. "Anyway, according to Mrs. Cranston's report, one told the other the punch stank—"

I don't think I want to hear this, thought Ashley.

"—so the other leaned forward to smell it—"

Uh. Oh.

Not that old trick!

"—and the one shoved the other's face into the bowl. I bet it was Paige who was the dunker," said Grammie.

Ohyes. The dunker would most definitely have been Paige.

"And Jessica was the dunkee," said Grammie.

"Donkey," mumbled Ed, who was sitting in the La-Z-Boy with his nose in the newspaper.

"But, like you guys say, Oh well!" Grammie sang out. "The news isn't all bad." She smiled a wicked little smile at Ashley. "The twins won't be there to drive you crazy at the party. So I guess you could say your fifty-cent piece may have just gotten a little luckier.

"Now. Back to business." She leaned very, very close to Ashley. She held the brushes on the mascara wand very near Ashley's eyeball. "This is lash thickening and lengthening—not that you need it. Blink."

Ashley slowly blinked her eyelashes across the mascara wand.

"Good. I see you found the twinkles."

"Mmmmm-hmmm," said Ashley. "But Grammie?"

"Blink!"

Ashley blinked again. "What about you and Phyllis going to the Shangri-La Room tonight?"

"No!" said Grammie in a stern voice. "Ab-so-lute-ly *not*! The last thing Phyllis and I need to do tonight is go to a Shangri-La Room. We're going to sit down right here when she gets back and map out a plan for the family, for 2000. Blink!"

Ashley blinked again.

"The girls will go straight to their rooms!"

They *will*?

Cool! thought Ashley.

"Ed will go next door and fix some hors d'oeuvres."

"I will?" said Ed.

"Every princely gentleman should be able to cook," whispered Grammie. "And run a vacuum," she added with a wink.

"Grammie?" said Ashley.

"Yes?"

"In case I forget—will you please put my diary in the twins' room? It's on my bed. Please make sure it stays open on the same page it's on right now. And put it on Paige's pillow. There's a little message written there . . ."

"For them? In *your* diary?"

"Ummm-hmmm."

"Okay. If you say so . . ."

"And—there's prune juice and frozen individual pizzas for them," added Ashley, "if they want a snack."

Grammie smiled a little. "Perfect!" she said. She tipped her head from side to side to admire her handiwork. "Stand up."

Ashley stood up.

Grammie stepped back and evaluated her, from her sparkling hair clips to the tips of her high-heel shoes. "Can you walk in those things?"

"Of course not," said Ashley. She wobbled her way across the rug. "How could anybody walk in these things?"

"Take them off and carefully put them in a potted plant the minute you walk in the door," suggested Grammie. "But don't leave one behind!"

"I won't."

"Those kicks are cute! And there's more than one Cinderella in town. I might like to borrow them sometime."

"You can."

Grammie turned to Ed. "Whaddya think of my fairy godkid?"

Ed looked over at Ashley. "I think she's great. And I think she's the spittin' image of her father."

"I do too." Grammie's eyes got a little misty as she looked at Ashley, standing in the light of the chandelier with her curls tumbling onto her shoulders.

"And I think her fairy godmother's great too," Ed added.

"Actually, I really *do* feel like Cinderella," said Ashley quietly.

"So do I," said Grammie. She walked over and patted Ed's shoulder. "You don't know about *my* fairy godmother. Yet!" she told him mysteriously.

Ed shifted his weight. "What's up with this chair? Oh, it's you." He pulled Froggy out from behind the cushion by one leg.

"Hey! You found him!" said Ashley. She took Froggy from Ed and gave Froggy a kiss.

And at that exact moment she heard the quiet ringing of the cell phone in her purse. She flung Froggy back in Ed's direction. She took the phone out of her purse and opened it. "Hello?"

"Hey," said Trevor. "We're outside."

"I'll be ready in just one minute," said Ashley.

"Want me to come up to the door?"

Ashley could hear the sounds of a football game in the background. "Whoa!" one of the guys called out.

"Turn it down," she heard Trevor say.

"EEEEyeah!" growled somebody.

"Turn it down!"

"EEEEyeah!" the guys growled in unison.

"Kyle brought his dad's *Football Hall of Fame* videos. Shut up!" Trevor yelled at the guys in the limo. The background noise grew softer.

"Yes," Ashley decided. "Come up."

Well, how else could she get down the stairs? Without Trevor helping her?

"Ed!" whispered Grammie. "Up you get!" Grammie dimmed the lights and took Ed's hand and led him through the kitchen doorway.

Ashley teetered over to the front door and opened it. She watched Trevor walk up the stairs—in his black tuxedo, white shirt and black bow tie. He never took his eyes off Ashley as he climbed the steps.

"Hey."

"Hey," said Ashley.

They stared at each other for a long time without saying anything.

Trevor was holding a small, square, clear plastic box.

He handed Ashley the box and she carefully opened it. Inside was a wrist corsage made of three pink rosebuds and baby's breath tied with a black velvet ribbon.

"It's a wristlet," said Trevor.

How *sweet*! thought Ashley. She took it out of the box and gave it a sniff. "Mmmmm. Thank you *so* much!"

Trevor helped guide her hand into the elastic wristband. "Awesome," he said, looking closely at her nails. The colors blended from blue to pink to peach. "I've seen a snowboard painted like that—at Ski and Sport."

"My gram painted them."

Ashley turned toward Grammie and Ed Anderson, who were peering out from behind the doorjamb. "This is Trevor," Ashley called to them.

"Hello, Trevor," said Ed as he and Grammie crossed the room. Ed tucked Froggy under his arm and shook hands with Trevor.

Ashley lifted her wrist so Grammie could have a smell.

"Lovely! What time will Ashley be home?" Grammie asked.

"What time do you want her to be home?" said Trevor.

"Well—you've got the phone," said Grammie quietly to Ashley. "What time did Phyllis say?"

"She didn't say for sure," said Ashley. "But she did say I could stay out past midnight. Kyle's aunt is driving the limo."

"She's the chaperone," added Trevor.

"Well, if you're going to be later than, say, one-thirty, call. We'll be up! Ed and I— we're going to watch the sun rise together. Okay, Ed?"

He nodded.

"With Phyllis," added Grammie. "As *our* chaperone. If she's not too tired."

"Okay," said Ashley.

Cool!

"Got your pager?" Grammie asked Trevor. "If we need to collect Ashley sooner, we'll page you."

Trevor told Ed the pager number and Ed wrote it down. "Did you want to come out and meet Kyle's aunt?" Trevor offered. "She's also a race car driver."

Ashley softly elbowed him.

"Well . . . ," said Ed.

"No," said Grammie. "We don't." She stepped on Ed's toe. "That won't be necessary."

"Where's Ashley's coat?" Ed asked.

"I don't need one."

"You'll freeze!" said Ed.

"No, I won't," said Ashley.

"It's December thirty-first!" said Ed.

Ashley and Grammie looked at each other. "Don't you have *something* you could throw on?" said Grammie.

"I suppose," said Ashley with a sigh. She opened the shopping bag Phyllis had thrown on the chair and peered in. Keeping her hands in the bag, she removed the tags from the remaining jacket. She folded it up inside itself, concealing the faux fur.

"Have fun," Grammie told them.

And they walked out the door.

Kyle's aunt, wearing a black tux and patent leather shoes, was waiting outside the car. She opened the back door for Ashley and Trevor and they squeezed in.

"Oh mygosh," was all Lily could think to say when she saw Ashley.

Evan, Kyle and Roland exchanged glances. Marshall gave Trevor a look.

Get this limo moving! thought Ashley.

Before Phyllis gets home. And stops in the middle of the street and honks and waves. And insists on meeting everybody. And says how cute the boys look in their tuxes. And says "What's up, fellas?"

Get me out of here! Ashley cried out to herself. She leaned down and poked her jacket under the seat.

Kyle's aunt pulled away from the curb. She did a K turn in the road, just past Ed Anderson's house.

On the way back down the street, Ashley could see headlights coming toward them. She could hear the low rumble of the station wagon's muffler as it approached. It paused just under a streetlight in anticipation of turning into Ashley's driveway.

Help! thought Ashley.

Kyle slid the window open that separated the backseat from the driver. "Aunt Janet. Isn't that a Chevy Nomad up ahead?"

"Ummm-hmmm—it's a fifty-five. Cool, huh?" She slowed down for a better look. "Or a fifty-six."

Kyle turned to Trevor. "Check out the Nomad."

Ashley held her breath.

"Sweet ride," said Trevor.

Aunt Janet beeped the horn and gave Phyllis a thumbs-up sign.

Yikes!

Phyllis beeped back.

"Stop. We want to get out and look at it," said Kyle.

No, we don't, thought Ashley. We really really *really* do not!

Aunt Janet checked her watch.

Marshall stood up through the moon roof. "We want your car!" he yelled to Phyllis.

Ashley cringed.

Marshall began drumming on the roof of the limo. "Bad car!" Marshall shouted.

Kyle dragged him back in and there was a brief wrestling match.

Ashley peered out the window. Phyllis was now pulling into the driveway.

"Boys?" said Aunt Janet as she started back down the street.

"Sorry," said Kyle.

The limo grew quiet.

For about one minute.

Kyle, Roland and Marshall grappled with the CD case briefly before agreeing on a CD. They played it at top volume—with Evan watching the football video on mute.

Ashley hoped Marshall wouldn't stand up again and yell and wave out of the top of the limo and bang on the roof.

And make a scene.

But none of the other kids seemed to care.

So maybe she hoped he would!

Relax, she told herself.

The clock on the VCR said 7:34. There were three more stops for the limo to make and three more unruly boys to pick up. Plus, it was a fifteen-minute drive to the west and then a winding mile up to the country club. Phyllis and the girls would be long gone from the party by the time the limo arrived.

Ashley hoped.

"After the party, maybe we can take the long way home," said Trevor. "Your friend Ana that I talked to told me she's staying out at the coast. With Emily. Do I know Emily?"

"Not yet," said Ashley.

"Ana said those guys are going to stay up all night and watch the sunrise," said Trevor.

"They are—with their families. They're having a bonfire on the beach."

"Do you know where?"

"Ummm-hmmm."

"Want to see if we can find them?"

"We can find them," said Ashley.

A slow song began to play, and it tamed the boys for a few minutes. The limo went from house to house. And—what a shame! Ashley and Trevor were forced to sit closer and closer together with each stop.

Good thing the limo wasn't a stretch!

White lights twinkled in the empty branches of the trees lining the road that wound to the top of the ridge, toward Ocean Crest. As they approached the entrance, lights marked the edges of the pavement and marked pathways that disappeared past bushes blooming in the darkness.

"Whoa! There's another Nomad!" said Kyle.

Ashley froze.

Just ahead, Phyllis was navigating the yacht. Ashley could make out the twins, both in the backseat, scowling.

With perfect timing, Ashley turned her face toward Trevor's—just as the limo and the Nomad squeaked past each other on the narrow pavement, going in opposite directions.

Don't look back, Ashley told herself. Only look forward. Her nose was very, very close to Trevor's face. His lips were open a little. She could see the bottoms of his two front teeth, and one had a small chip in it.

A perfect chip.

"Thanks for the flowers," she whispered.

Trevor looked down at her wrist.

Then, careful not to crush the rosebuds, he moved his hand into Ashley's hand and held it. Nobody noticed. Or if they did, they didn't seem to notice.

Ashley could see that the parking lot and the

dark, grassy hillsides were filled with white canvas tents, strung with lights—as if a carnival were going on. Each tent was serving a different kind of food. Ohmygosh! There was even a See's candy tent!

The limo idled near where a woman in an orange dress was standing behind a stainless steel machine, twirling cotton candy onto a white paper baton.

Trevor slumped down in the seat.

The woman held the cotton candy in front of her like a cloud.

A man was strolling among the guests and tents, passing out glowing plastic roses. He took the cotton candy from the woman and gave her a rose. And yikes! She stole a kiss.

"I cannot believe my mom kissed my dad fully in view of the public," grumbled Trevor.

Ashley smiled to herself.

Cool!

And in an orange dress, no less!

Evan ejected his Hall of Fame video; Kyle ejected his CD, slid it into the case and zipped the case closed.

Now Ashley could hear a band playing over outdoor speakers. The deejay, from a local radio station, had set up his KIRK THOMSON sign outside the entrance and was standing in front of it, signing autographs. Ashley saw Brittany, Mara—also Laura, Angie, Rachel and Kortney! And Kesha—from drama class! And Michelle! Swarming around him.

Ashley could see wet splotches on the lapel of Kirk Thomson's jacket. Apparently he'd dabbed off the barbecue sauce.

This splotched-suited man was a celebrity. And a mighty cute one, Ashley noticed. To think, she thought with a sigh—it was *my little sisters* who beaned him with chicken wings.

Nobody saw this! She assured herself. And now—the twins had simply . . . vanished!

Ashley could have kissed them, she was so happy!

Soon Kirk's lapel would dry. Ashley hoped. For his sake—and for hers. Although really, why should she care what the twins had done?

She wasn't them.

They weren't her.

One day they'd grow up, and they'd all be real sisters to each other. Maybe even sometime in the twenty-first century!

"There's Ben at the burger tent," said Marshall. "And Mark and Jason." He rolled down the window. "What up," he called across the grass.

They paid no attention to him. Ben tipped his head back and dropped some fries into his mouth. Mark and Jason were apparently in a contest, trying to impress two girls, Katie and Christine, who watched with disgust as the boys each tried to eat a burger in one bite.

"And Sam. And Glen and Jonathan," said Kyle. These three were scarfing pizza, tipping forward to keep from dropping cheese down their shirts. "And John. And Josh! Hey!" Kyle shouted out the window.

"Did anybody bring a football?" Roland wondered out loud.

"I hope not," Lily told him.

"Is there a big-screen TV inside?" Kyle asked.

"Yeah," said Trevor.

"Think they'd let us show *Greatest Plays*?"

"Yeah," said Trevor.

Lily and Ashley made eye contact.

"What about our snowboarding video!" said Evan.

"Yeah," said Trevor.

"Well, I'll drop you off—and then park over

there," said Aunt Janet. "Get the videos later. Kyle? Score me a burger and some fries." She pulled to the curb and got out and opened the door. The boys politely waited for Lily to slide out of the car, then piled out. Evan tackled Kyle and they rolled into a bush.

Roland dove on top of both of them.

Trevor got out and looked back in at Ashley. He held out his hand and she took it and wobbled out onto the flagstone sidewalk.

"You cold?"

"A little," said Ashley.

Trevor took off his jacket and put it around her shoulders. He put his arm around her and held her close. He looked at her neck. "You're sparkling."

"It's Fairy Dust."

"I believe it."

Trevor checked out Ashley's hair. "There's dragonflies all over you." He looked at her earlobe. "There's one on your ear."

Ashley put her hand on her throat and found the dragonfly on the silver chain. She held it out a little so Trevor could see.

"You smell good," said Trevor.

"It's GUESS?."

"I give up."

"Millennium—by GUESS?."

"I give up!"

Ashley said nothing. She searched Trevor's eyes, then looked past his shoulder. The sky was black.

A fingernail moon was hanging in a treetop. The night was sizzling with stars.

About the Author

Mavis Jukes won a Newbery Honor Book citation for *Like Jake and Me* and is the author of numerous books for children and young adults, including *Blackberries in the Dark, Expecting the Unexpected, Planning the Impossible* and *It's a Girl Thing*. She lives with her husband and daughters in Northern California.